A Kiss of Promise
Elaine Violette

A Kiss of Promise
Copyright 2016 EV's Books
ISBN: 978-0-9966821-6-9

Cover Art by Harris Channing

Dedication

For my mom, Millie Santos Noyes, who passed away on September 22, 2014. She taught me through example the true meaning of patience, perseverance, and faith. To my husband, children, and grandchildren who are the loves of my life.

Prologue
One year ago

ALAINA'S HANDS trembled as she held what appeared to be the proof of her father's villainy. Kneeling on the Oriental rug in his private library, she fingered Lord Blackstone's seal embossed on the ancient tome. Martin and York Blackstone had alleged that a set of four books, valuable collectors' items, had disappeared from their father's library before he was accused of treason. One of the stolen books, later found to be concealing secret information meant for the French, became the evidence that convicted their father of treason and sent him to prison for life.

Her own father was Lord Blackstone's accuser. For his loyalty to the Crown, he was granted the Blackstone estate, her home for the past fifteen years, a home where her father's cruel domination suffocated any possibility for love or devotion toward him.

Staring at the aged book, she dwelled on the Blackstone brothers' adamant claims they'd made to her and to her brother during a clandestine meeting they'd orchestrated. She recollected the anguish mixed with rage she saw in their eyes when they spoke of their mother's bravery and sacrifice. Knowing of her husband's pride over possessing this one set of prized religious tomes, she'd planned to slip the collection away before the estate was confiscated. When their mother searched his library, she discovered that the collection was missing.

Their mother, now deceased, believed they'd been stolen by a housemaid who had worked for them for only a short time and mysteriously disappeared without notice a few days before her husband's arrest. When the authorities came, all was seized and she and her children relegated to the streets. Their mother managed to conceal some jewelry and pound notes she'd sewn into her cape and her two boys' coats. It was barely enough to rent a small apartment in London until the money ran out. After their mother who had found a job in a workhouse died, the two boys were left to survive on their own.

Alaina pressed one hand to her breast as the horror they must have gone through gripped her heart. Young children, accustomed to a life of quality, orphaned, and forced to eke out an existence with beggars and thieves. How did they manage to survive? Yet the brothers returned, strong, defiant, and prepared to avenge their father's persecution.

Martin, the younger brother, had captured her heart when they were small children and neighbors, playing together near their families' joint properties. He'd tease her mercilessly, she remembered, but she still followed after him for even a smidgeon of attention. She'd been too young to understand when one day the family simply vanished without explanation. She'd pouted silently for weeks, waiting for the brothers to return. She never saw them again, until a few weeks ago.

Shaking herself from her bleak contemplations, she gathered up her skirts and rose to her feet, still holding the tome. She had to get out of the library before her father returned. She would take this one with her and show it to the Blackstone brothers. Perhaps they were mistaken, but the collection was just as the men described. Unlike her father's other prized books, these were not on display, but hidden, and there were just three of them left.

Setting the tome aside on the rug, she climbed the wooden ladder that stood against the mahogany wall of books and eyed the remaining two. She shivered at the thought of the missing one that had led to the family's ruin.

Did the remaining books hold the proof of a man's innocence and of another's guilt? Grief and tension gripped her as she stepped down. She gathered a few of the books she'd strewn across the floor, books that had concealed the volumes on a secret shelf for over fifteen years. Climbing back up, she returned them to their previous position, stepped down, gathered the few remaining books and did the same.

"Alaina, what have you done?"

The last book dropped from her hand as one foot slipped from the ladder rung. She grasped the side rails to stop her fall. Taking a shaky breath, she twisted her body in the direction of her father's cold voice.

Lord Craymore stood just within the library door, rage distorting his features.

"I...came to borrow a book." She forced the words out as she descended the ladder. Feeling her father's eyes blazing at her, she knelt down and picked up the book she'd dropped. The few seconds gave her time to collect her wits and relax her facial muscles. He mustn't see her fear.

"And what did you find, Alaina?"

The chill in his voice sent ripples down her spine. She had no idea what she held in her hand. She read the title. Relief flooded her. "Alexander Pope, Father. I enjoy his poetry. I hope you don't mind." She opened it and smoothed her hand across a page. "I'd like to take it with me to London, to read along the way." She prayed that she sounded convincing. Her father's frozen expression unnerved her. "I should get back to my packing."

She walked toward the door, praying he'd step aside. He said nothing, just stood like a stone. She forced her body to maintain poise and her expression, casual indifference. When she was a foot from him, he grabbed her forearm, tightening his grip and pulled her toward him.

Pain shot through her arm.

"You know I don't approve of you in here when I am not present."

"I had no idea when you would return and I wanted to finish packing."

"Father?" Her brother, Richard, appeared at the door, his eyes focused on his father's fist clenching Alaina's arm.

"I found her snooping about."

"I only wanted to borrow a book for travel."

Lord Craymore drew her arm closer before releasing her. "Get out of here. I have work to do. Richard, we need to talk."

Alaina rushed from the room, rubbing her bruised arm, but not before giving her brother a warning nod. Hurrying through the hall, she lifted her skirts and ran up the staircase to her bedchamber, collapsing into a chair.

Catching her breath, her mind reeled with the reality of her discovery. She hadn't wanted to believe the brothers' charges—that her father possessed the books that had been stolen, then used to frame Lord Blackstone. Over the years, her father had often bragged about his part in the man's downfall. He'd brought a traitor to justice and the king had rewarded him for his loyalty. When they'd moved into the accused traitor's estate she'd been too young to understand the implications.

Blackstone's sons, York and Martin, now grown, had returned to prove their father's innocence. They'd insisted that the treasonous message from France concealed in one of his books had been placed there after it was stolen. Their mother had pleaded with the court, telling of the missing tomes, but she had been ignored. It was Alaina's father who had urged the authorities to investigate Lord Blackstone and it was his damaging testimony that had been accepted by the courts. Seeing Martin again fifteen years later brought back the memories of her childhood.

The image of him as a young boy had little comparison to the tall, broad-shouldered, and ruggedly handsome man he'd become. She'd been surprised at her reaction to him, at first wariness and after a time, attraction. She remembered the moment when he grinned at her and she was taken back to years past and to the last time she'd seen him, a grinning, mischievous nine-year-old. Her heart warmed in his presence, though she'd felt shy at first and then confused at their sudden appearance and declarations.

She sat back in the chair, rubbing her bruised arm when her hand flew to her mouth. *Oh, dear God.* She'd forgotten the tome she'd set aside. Where had she placed it? She closed her eyes and tried to recreate that moment. She envisioned the room, the dark mahogany wood of the bookcases, the heavy velvet drapes that covered the long windows, her father's desk and the two leather chairs that faced it. She'd left it on the rug, near the curtains. Would the small worn book blend in with the print of the dark-burgundy rug? It might, at least for a time, she thought, or was she just wishing it so?

She imagined him talking to her brother about business, perhaps rifling through the papers on his desk, his mind on his work. His desk was out of view of where she was certain she'd forgotten the small book. If she could think of a reason to go back, draw his attention to other matter... No, not while he was still in the library. She recalled the rage in his eyes. She had to be patient and wait for him to leave.

She paced back and forth as the minutes wore on, even tried to go back to her packing, but all she could think about was the lone book that lay on the floor and what her father's reaction would be if he found it.

In society, her father was respected as a wealthy aristocrat and a shrewd businessman. Only a very few had the discernment to see beyond the façade. In their home, he was a tyrant, cruel to his wife, now deceased, and demanding of his children's obedience in all matters. Only his son and heir received her father's regard. He wanted Richard to follow in his footsteps and for a time her brother had savored his favored status. Thankfully, he was also his mother's son and had eventually realized his father's duplicity.

Richard was Alaina's rock and her protector from her father's sometimes deranged insinuations and ridicule. In her father's eyes, she was an annoyance, a burden that he hoped to marry off soon.

When the Blackstone brothers appeared, Richard had questioned their story at first, but they were not to be deterred from their mission. Both she and Richard had come to admire their tenacity and sympathized with the hardships they'd endured. Now she had discovered possible proof of their claim.

She needed to talk to her brother and tell him what she'd found. He would know what to do.

Her thoughts were interrupted by a knock on the door. She jolted from her chair while fear clutched at her chest.

"Who is it?"

"It's Baldwin, Miss."

Alaina exhaled a relieved breath.

She opened the door to find their butler holding a small tray.

"Your father asked me to bring you some tea."

She gaped at the servant. Her father seldom showed courtesy toward her.

"He believes he has upset you, Miss. Shall I set it down?"

She knew the servants were aware of her father's mood changes and understood Baldwin's sympathetic expression.

"I'll take it. Is my father still in the library with Richard?"

"Your brother left a short time ago. Your father is at his desk."

"Thank you, Baldwin." She took the tray from his hands and carried it into the room.

Richard had witnessed her father's anger in the library. Had her father appeased him by offering a gesture of apology? It was the only reason she could think of that would cause him to consider her distress.

She set the tray down and poured a cup of tea but pushed it aside. She had to get that book before he discovered it. She began to pace again. *He most likely won't leave the library until dinner unless I can draw him away.*

Desperate, she searched her mind for a plan. Nothing seemed plausible. She had no choice. She had to go down to the library, perhaps ask him questions concerning their trip to London in a few days. Did she dare ask for another book? If she could walk casually over to the spot where he'd found her, she might be able to cover the book with her long skirt, kick it under the drapes and retrieve it later.

Her rambling thoughts were interrupted by a sound in the hallway. She realized she'd left her door partially ajar. The door swung open and her father walked in, closing it behind him.

"Father?"

Lord Craymore, who never entered her bedchamber, wore a snide grin, his eyes cold and hard. "Did you miss something, Alaina?"

Her mouth dropped when she saw the worn tome in his clenched hand. "I don't know what you mean. It must have fallen from the shelf."

"Fallen? Remarkable considering that it was quite hidden. I assume you looked at it?"

"No, I…"

He stepped forward and clutched her shoulders. "Don't *lie* to me. How did you know about them?"

"I didn't. I was just—"

"Stop!" He slapped her hard across the face. She cringed and tried to pull away, her cheek burning from the blow, but he held her fast. He pushed her against one of the tall posters of her bed, her back digging into its ornate curves.

He gripped her chin and forced her to look at him, his voice low and menacing, the book he held jabbed into her shoulder. "I have wanted to share my little secret, a secret of which I am quite proud. When I discovered this prized volume on the floor where you'd been probing about, I decided it was time to acknowledge my feat. Look at me!"

She focused on eyes that appeared crazed.

"Better. I just told your brother. I know he is loyal to me. He understands the importance of protecting what will be his someday. You, on the other hand, I cannot trust. You are too much like your mother, unable to understand what a man must do to gain what he deserves and to *keep* what belongs to him."

"Father, please. You're hurting me."

"You are my daughter. You belong to me, just like everything else on this estate. Stop struggling. Like all women, you are weak." He looked at a side table where she'd set the teapot. "Did you drink your tea? I told Cook to add some laudanum for your distress. All my servants do as I ask. It will be completely understandable when they find you at the bottom of the stairs. You became groggy and instead of napping as you should, you tried to descend the stairs and you fell. I will be appropriately distraught."

"Father, no." She could barely get the words out. His hand lowered to her throat, making it difficult for her to breathe.

"You will *listen* to me. You know that this estate was granted to me by the king in exchange for my loyalty. But how did you know of the books? Never mind, it's unimportant. Unfortunately, I'll need to destroy them now. Such a shame."

"I didn't—"

"You didn't know that they were stolen from Blackstone and used to seal his fate? You see, Lord Blackstone called me a coward. Unforgivable. I refused his orders to go into a battle against Napoleon's forces. I believed it to be a hopeless charge. He discredited me, took all the war honors for himself. I simply found a way to get even."

Alaina tried to turn her head away from the viciousness in his voice. She thought of the gun in her dresser that her brother had given her for protection. If only she could free herself. She tried to pull away.

"I said look at me!" He jerked her face back to his. "It's time you knew the truth. I found a foolish servant willing to steal the volumes if I would pay her passage to America. Easily done. Then I paid an even more foolish Frenchman to deliver a treasonous message to Lord Blackstone, concealed in one of his own books. Blackstone arrived at the London docks, thinking that he was picking up a treasured manuscript to add to his collection. I alerted the authorities. They were in wait. They took him into custody once the transfer was made. I even had the Frenchman drowned so he couldn't be questioned later." He grinned. "Don't look so horrified. It was a perfect crime and I was honored for it." Craymore sneered as he dragged her forward, closer to the door.

"I was treated like royalty for turning in a traitor to the king, all with false evidence. I am *no* coward. Blackstone rotted in prison, all by my doing. Perhaps I should have destroyed the books long ago, but I couldn't part with them. They are priceless and a proud reminder of my feat."

Alaina tried to scream, but his hand pressed against her mouth.

"No one will hear you. I've sent everyone off on errands and you, my dear, were kind enough to give your maid the afternoon off. How convenient. Now, you know too much. You must die."

He twisted her about until her back was pressed against his chest. He tightened one arm around her waist, his other hand still covering her mouth. She struggled, trying to grab at the doorjamb, but he pulled her through.

"Fighting is useless, Alaina. It will be over soon," he whispered in her ear.

She beat his arms with her fists and tried to pull his hand from her mouth. She could barely breathe and only a muffled scream could escape.

She was going to die.

"Agh." Craymore's grip loosened as an arm went around his neck, choking him. "Let her go!" Richard yelled. He dragged his father farther into the hallway, disengaging him from his sister.

Alaina watched in horror as her father fought against his son's grip, nearly freeing himself until the butt of a gun slammed down on his brow. She looked up to see York Blackstone holding a gun in the air as her father fell to the floor, his face twisting in anguish.

"Alaina, are you all right?"

She recognized the voice. She looked beyond York. Martin, his brother, reached out a hand to her, his face unshaven and creased with concern. *Martin.* Their eyes met.

"Alaina?" Martin shouted, causing her to shake off the sense of unreality that seemed to be drawing her in, suffocating her.

"Yes, yes, I can't believe you're here." She looked down at her father. "He was going to kill me."

Her father groaned as he tried to get to his knees. One of his arms reached for a baluster, the other pulled at his coat that appeared snagged beneath his knees.

York kicked at his outstretched arm. Her father crumpled back to the floor, cursing. Her brother pulled her clear of her father's grasp, wrapping an arm around her.

"Richard, I found the books. He knew."

"Don't try to talk. Father told me everything. He bragged as if he'd accomplished some great deed," Richard spat, glaring at his father who now appeared barely conscious. "He thought I'd marvel at his accomplishment. He's crazed."

"We'll take him to the library," York muttered. "Martin, grab his other arm."

Alaina, her shoulders pressed against the hallway wall, watched as York and Martin lifted her father by his armpits and dragged him down the stairs.

Richard stayed behind. "Go to your room and rest."

"He was going to push me down the stairs and say it was an accident," she murmured. "He had the tea laced with laudanum so he could blame my death on drowsiness."

"No need to relive it now," Richard said gently, his hand touching her cheek that was still raw from her father's slap. "Father sent me to the stalls and told me to have our horses saddled. He ordered tea for you as if your discovery was of little concern to him. I watched him go back to work. He gave no hint of evil intent. I thought I had time to find York and Martin. You and I both know they were watching the house, looking for an opportunity to search without Father about. You should not have tried to do it on your own. It was too dangerous."

Alaina nodded, her need to find the truth nearly causing her own death.

"When I told them what happened, they refused to wait any longer. Thank God, we arrived in time. Forgive me, Alaina. I should never have left. I underestimated the depth of his cruelty."

"You're not to blame. We could never have imagined that he would kill and with no regret. If you could have seen the mocking leer on his face."

"Try to wipe it from your mind," Richard urged. "He thought he could take me into his confidence, expected that I would congratulate him. His depravity has led to madness. Now the Blackstones are ready for their revenge. I need to go downstairs and see what's happening. Go to your room. I want you protected."

Alaina reached for her brother's hand. "I'm safe now. Go." She waved him away. "Truly, I am all right," she said when he didn't move. He nodded and disappeared down the stairs.

You are my daughter. You belong to me...you must die. The words sliced through her like shards of glass. She pressed a hand to her heart, wanting to contain the horror she felt at her father's words.

She walked into her bedchamber, still feeling dazed. She picked up the tome that had fallen when her father dragged her to the door and set it down on her nightstand. She hesitated then with trembling hands, she opened the drawer that concealed her gun and stared at it, finally lifting it out. She tucked it in the pocket of her skirt. She couldn't hide in here while her brother dealt with their father and she wanted — needed — protection.

She left her room and walked down the stairs to the library. When she reached the opened door, she peered in, feeling like a character in a tragic play, her mind and body numbed.

Her father sat in one of his leather chairs that had been turned about and now faced the door. His usually neatly combed gray hair was matted with blood and plastered to his forehead. He looked like a feeble old man who'd aged twenty years. She stood motionless, out of view, watching and listening. York stood before him.

"Blackstone? What are you doing in my house?" her father gasped in a gruff voice. "Richard, call the authorities. Grab him!"

York drew closer.

"You were supposed to have died in prison. You've returned too late. It's all mine now."

Dear God, my father believes him to be Lord Blackstone.

"No, it can't be," her father continued ranting. "I made sure you were locked up long enough to kill any man. Richard, help me to my room," he growled. "I must be hallucinating. Richard, get me out of here!"

Her brother drew closer and stood before him. "It is Lord Blackstone's son, Father," he said in a strong voice. "He's come to claim what is rightfully his. He is not an illusion."

"Rightfully his? What have you done?" Craymore snarled before falling into a fit of coughing. He grappled in his pocket, pulled out a handkerchief, bent low and coughed into it. The men turned to each other, mumbling something Alaina couldn't hear. Her eyes returned to her father. She watched as he lowered his other hand into his boot, his fingers clawing, scratching. In seconds, she saw the glint of metal and gaped as her father raised a small revolver and pointed it at Richard.

"Richard!"

Her brother turned toward her, just as her father pulled the trigger. Richard fell back into York. In an instant, Alaina pulled the gun from her pocket. The shot rang across the room. She dropped her hand that held the smoldering pistol, her eyes fixed on her father who seemed to be staring through her before his body went limp. The gun dangling from her fingers fell to the floor.

"Richard?" She sobbed, ran into the room and knelt by her brother.

"It's my arm, Alaina, I'm all right." He forced a shaky smile. "This time *you* saved me."

York pulled Alaina away while Martin helped Richard stand before settling him in a chair. York checked Craymore's pulse. "It's over, he's dead." His voice sounded hollow and distant.

"I killed him, my own father," Alaina whispered, her eyes glazed and her lower lip trembling.

"Get her out of here," York ordered. "We need to send for the authorities. No need to have her involved."

"No, Richard needs a doctor...'" She tried to say more but her stomach heaved as she gazed at her father's body and saw blood dripping onto the rug. She grasped her throat, afraid she would be sick. "I murdered my father."

"Alaina, you mustn't be here when they come." Her brother's words were the last thing she remembered before a wave of dizziness overpowered her and her world turned dark.

Chapter One

ALAINA STOOD in front of her bedroom mirror, staring at her reflection. The lavender dress she wore was a couple of years old, but it should appease her benefactor. Lady Cornelia Henley or Aunt Cornelia, as she preferred to be called, had insisted that she cast off the darker shades of mourning now that a year had passed since her father's death.

Whatever she wore made little difference. She seldom left the house, except on an errand or a brief shopping trip. Invitations sent to Aunt Cornelia seldom included her. Even when she'd been invited, she found it was more out of the hostess's curiosity at her condition or to give her other guests someone to whisper about. The Blackstone-Craymore scandal remained fresh in everyone's mind and embellished stories that held little likeness to the true circumstances continued to circulate. No one knew that she'd been the one who'd shot her father to death or that she still woke up shivering in the night at the enormity of her crime.

She held that truth in her heart, but her family name had been dragged through the dirt, her father had wrongfully accused a noble aristocrat of treason out of greed, and many believed that the Craymore children had been a party to it, simply because of their name.

Alaina had feared that Cornelia would pay dearly for taking her in, but thankfully, the sprightly elderly lady refused to let others' judgments concern her. She'd been a calming influence throughout the scandal and knew all the sordid details since Marielle Henley, Alaina's oldest and dearest friend, was Cornelia's niece and York Blackstone's wife.

Marielle and York had fallen in love during his struggle to regain his inheritance. Aunt Cornelia was privy to all the details. Her niece and her husband were now settled into the Blackstone estate, happily wed and with a new baby girl. It was Marielle who had approached her aunt concerning Alaina's welfare after her home had been confiscated by the authorities. Cornelia had opened her heart and her home to her despite her family's fall from grace. How could she ever thank her?

She'd agreed to the change in wardrobe, but refused the invitation to visit York and Marielle, though Cornelia encouraged her to go. She wasn't ready to return to the estate that had been her childhood home as well as the place where her father had died at her hands. Further, York only reminded her of his younger brother, Martin, since the two looked so much alike. Once the court proceedings were over and the estate returned to York Blackstone, its rightful heir, she and Martin spent time together under Aunt Cornelia's watchful eye. Martin had been understanding and had helped to shield her from being questioned by authorities.

She could never forget his kindness or his gray eyes searching hers nor the few minutes that they were alone on the Blackstone veranda, when he reached out to her and held her. They'd been talking about putting the worst of the past aside. He had encouraged her to hold her head high when society cast her off as the child of a tyrant.

Then he'd kissed her, not a kiss between friends, but in her memory of the moment, a kiss of promise. He'd made her feel whole and young and hopeful when her insides felt bruised and shamed.

Oh, Martin, I hoped for too much. How could I have expected that you would fall in love with the daughter of the man who destroyed your family? She'd always be a reminder of the years he and his brother had spent trying to survive when he should have been enjoying a life of regal dignity. *No wonder you chose to leave England and find adventure in America.* She tried to understand but still felt devastated that he'd left unexpectedly, and without taking the time to visit her and say goodbye.

He'd sent her one letter after arriving in Boston. She'd read it over so many times that it was barely legible now. He had promised he'd return to London one day, but there was no mention of returning to her. What else could she have expected?

She fisted a hand to her lips to stop the anguishing memories and stifle the anger at the unfairness of it all. She'd allowed herself to believe that Martin's kiss meant something more. No doubt he knew that she'd adored him when they were children, but she'd been a ponytailed nuisance. The kiss obviously didn't mean the same to a man anxious to leave a tragic past behind.

She thought of her brother. At least Richard had been able to reestablish himself in business over the past few months. Fortunately for him, a man's past was more easily forgiven than a woman's. How could she not be happy for him? He'd been everything to her after their mother's death and he'd been her protector against her father's abusive tirades.

Aunt Cornelia's voice from the other side of her bedroom door shook her out of her dismal musings. "Alaina?"

"Come in, I was just about to come down."

"My, my, don't you look lovely," Cornelia said as she entered. "That color becomes you."

"I thought you would be pleased." Alaina tried to return her benefactor's cheery smile. "I so appreciate everything you've done for me, Aunt Cornelia. And it's been a year that I have taken advantage of your generosity. I wish I could repay you in some way." She reached out and gave the older woman a gentle hug before turning away. She walked the few steps to her window and pushed the curtain aside, staring out into the street. "If I could find a position, perhaps as a governess, out of London, where my family's disgrace might be unknown, I would no longer be a burden to you."

"You have never been a burden. Please, never say that again."

Alaina continued to look away as tears threatened. Her previous thoughts only increased the gratitude she felt for the dear woman. "I have caused you undeserved criticism, even from your closest friends."

"Nonsense. I have enjoyed your company. I may have originally taken you in at my niece's request, but I have benefitted by your companionship. I have come to love you like a daughter. I am well aware of the unfairness of society's judgment. I refuse to be party to it and cater to others' favor, friends or acquaintances. I am too old to concern myself with their pettiness."

Cornelia waved a hand in the air as if to brush off their small-mindedness. "You have not deserved their cruelty, Alaina. You have a heart full of unselfish love. I know how you cared for your mother during her illness and your allegiance to your brother. In my eyes, you have paid the heaviest of prices for your father's crimes for too long. I pray in time, the shroud many have placed over you will be removed. Perhaps we need another scandal to fill their ears."

Alaina chuckled at Cornelia's attempt at humor while her heart burst with overflowing gratitude at her vehement loyalty.

"How can I ever thank you?"

"By allowing me to take you shopping for some new gowns. Styles do change, you know. And I do want you to come along to more events with me. You must admit that when you have accompanied me, gentlemen have attempted conversation with you. I remember well that young man, Mr. Barclay, Lady Townsend's nephew. He's asked if he could visit. He had no intention of visiting me, young lady, but you have wanted no male attention. Society has been cruel, but time heals and you are too lovely, my dear, for handsome gentlemen to stay away."

Alaina smiled tolerantly at her. The dear woman never gave up. She couldn't share her feelings for Martin with her. They were too deep and too precious. She needed to hold her longings close to her heart.

"My goodness, I am going on and almost forgot to tell you that your friend, Priscilla Dunfly, has arrived. Did you expect her?" Cornelia asked, her chin jutting out just enough to display her disfavor of Alaina's friend.

"No, but as you know, Priscilla has a tendency to stop in without notice."

"Yes, I have noticed."

"It has been nice to make a new friend," Alaina said gently, knowing that Cornelia had not taken well to Priscilla, a young widow Alaina had met while out for a walk a couple of months earlier.

"You are quite right, my dear. I should not judge her." Cornelia looked down at her small, wrinkled hands now clasped tightly to her waist, her posture revealing contrariness. "It is just that she seems to be overzealous in her desire to befriend you — not that you do not deserve to have many friends. I also noticed that she had her eyes on your brother Richard when he arrived during one of her visits."

"Are you suggesting that her continued friendship with me might have some ulterior motive, perhaps to get closer to my brother?"

Cornelia shrugged. "No doubt she enjoys your company and that may be all there is to it. I simply question her overzealousness in befriending you. She is a widow with a questionable reputation, I dare say. Your brother is extremely handsome and available. A close relationship with his sister is advantageous to that end. Perhaps she hopes that you will encourage a relationship between them." Cornelia smoothed the lace that edged the cuff of her long sleeves. "I do want you to make friends, Alaina, there's just something about her that disturbs me." Aunt Cornelia grew quiet before continuing. "Well, I am off to my tea. Thomas and Edith are here if you need anything, my dear."

"HOW NICE of you to stop in," Alaina said as she walked into the parlor to greet Priscilla.

"Alaina, you have finally shed those dreary dresses. You look beautiful."

"Thank you. I welcome your visit though I admit I am surprised to see you again so soon. I fear I may have little to talk about. My days are quite mundane."

"I desired some cultured conversation," Priscilla said, untying her frilly yellow bonnet. "Please come and sit. I was forced to spend the morning with that dreadfully boring Lady Dresden. I feel wrung out from her repetitive stories and woeful complaining about her husband," she said while tossing her bonnet aside. "She should accept that he has a mistress, most do. Honestly, you would think she'd be happy that he leaves her be. With his looks I would be on my knees thanking God for finding him a woman who'd keep him out of my bed."

Alaina sat beside her and listened patiently to her friend's dramatic outpouring.

"What she ever saw in him in the first place is beyond me, though no doubt his title had something to do with it. She did nothing but complain about him even before she found out about his affair."

Alaina smiled at her friend's chatter. Priscilla seldom allowed a moment's pause in conversation or accepted a refusal without pouting for effect. "How delightful you are. Your visit has brightened my day."

"Excuse me, Miss Alaina." The butler stood at the door of the drawing room.

"Yes, Thomas?"

"A gentleman is here to see you. A Mr. Harrington."

"A gentleman?"

She looked at Priscilla who, to her surprise, made no comment. Instead she seemed more concerned with straightening the ruffles on her skirt.

"I have no idea who Mr. Harrington is and I received no calling card," Alaina said, rising from her seat. "Perhaps another unfinished affair of my late father. I'll go and see what he wants and send him on his way. Richard insists on taking care of all unfinished business and he is out of London for the next couple of weeks." Alaina turned to leave.

Priscilla popped up from her seat. "Oh, no, please invite him in. I...know him."

"You know him?"

"Yes, we've met on a number of occasions."

Alaina noted that Priscilla appeared suddenly on edge. Her earlier conversation with Cornelia popped into her mind. *He may be someone Priscilla has an interest in as well.*

"If it's a business call, it may be tedious. Perhaps I should see him alone." She took a few steps to the door.

"I shall leave immediately if it appears I am intruding on business not of my concern, I promise."

Priscilla almost appeared to be pleading and did not follow her as Alaina had expected. Instead, she returned to her seat.

"If you insist," Alaina said finally, feeling uncomfortable at her friend's odd behavior but not certain how else to deal with her at the moment.

"Please show him in, Thomas."

She returned to her own seat and before she could ask Priscilla how she was acquainted with the visitor, the gentleman appeared.

"Mr. Phillip Harrington," Thomas announced. Alaina stayed seated as Harrington entered the drawing room. She couldn't help but notice that he was quite handsome—tall and slim, though she noted a severe tightness about his mouth that she found unflattering. She thought he might be close to thirty-five. He was well dressed in a single-breasted waistcoat in a subtle taupe with darker-brown trousers. His neckcloth, snow-white, was neatly tied without undue starch. Quite impressive. *His good looks must be the reason for Priscilla's desire to be present.*

"Miss Craymore, it is a pleasure to see you once again," Harrington said as he stopped a few feet from her, bowing slightly, and ignoring Priscilla.

"Once again? I am afraid you are mistaken. I don't believe I have made your acquaintance before."

"You were a mere child when I visited your father. Unfortunately, I needed to return to America soon after. You were extremely lovely then. You have grown into an even more beautiful woman."

Alaina's cheeks flushed. It had been a long time since a man complimented her appearance. Mr. Harrington was a flatterer. Still, there was something about him that made her uneasy. Perhaps it was his connection to her father that disturbed her. "I understand you and Mrs. Dunfly are acquainted."

Priscilla sat stone still, staring at Harrington while he simply nodded.

Alaina didn't know what to make of it. She felt uncomfortable talking about business in front of Priscilla and her friend made no move to lessen the strained atmosphere. "Mr. Harrington, you mentioned my father. If this concerns—"

"I would like you to see this as a social call," he interrupted. "A long overdue one, I am afraid. Do you mind if I have a seat?"

"Of course." She waved toward a chair near the settee that she and Priscilla shared. She glanced at Priscilla who looked tense, her lips clamped together and her eyes averted.

"And the reason for your visit?" Alaina asked, deciding to get it over with so he would be on his way. She wanted to question Priscilla about her peculiar behavior, but not in front of this stranger.

"I realize that I have been errant in not contacting you sooner or courting you properly but I have lived in America for the past few years."

"Courting me? You are extremely forward, Mr. Harrington, as well as improper. I do not even know you. Furthermore, I have a guest."

"Alaina," Priscilla interrupted. "I think you need to allow Mr. Harrington to explain."

Alaina looked from one to the other. "What is this all about?"

"Please." Priscilla reached out a hand and urged her to settle back.

Harrington rested his elbows on the arms of his chair and folded his hands. "I asked Mrs. Dunfly to be here today since I was unaware of how you would take the news I have to present. I thought her presence might be a comfort to you in case your father did not tell you about our contract."

"My father? He has been deceased for over a year."

"Yes, I do offer my condolences. I am disappointed, however, that he did not see fit to tell you of our signed agreement."

Alaina's body tensed. Just the mention of her father brought painful memories. She didn't know if she had the strength to know any more of her father's dealings.

Harrington removed a folded sheet of paper

from his coat. "I fear that this will come as a shock to you. The contract was drawn up over five years ago." He paused long enough for Alaina to lose her patience.

"Mr. Harrington," Alaina held out her hand.

Harrington gave her the paper and sat back, obviously waiting for her reaction.

Alaina unfolded the aged and wrinkled document, examined it, saw her father's seal and signature and began to read. She stopped suddenly and drew in a ragged breath. "Betrothed?" The word struck her like a blow.

"I see that this is truly a surprise," Harrington said, wearing a look of concern.

"This is outrageous. You certainly do not expect me to honor this." Alaina tossed the paper aside and rose from her seat. She nearly laughed aloud. Hadn't her father done enough to belittle her as a woman? Now, even in his grave, he could still have power over her life. Only an hour before she'd been thinking of Martin, wishing that like York and Marielle, they could have had a future together. That he would love her, miss her, return to her. How foolish to think she'd ever be free from her father's tyranny.

Harrington rose from the chair to retrieve the discarded document. "I had no idea your father hadn't discussed our contract."

Alaina's insides churned, not just with the shock, but with tremendous sadness. She'd tried to place her father in a different light after his death, even at times attempted to have mercy, to try to understand his need to claim what wasn't his. But once again she was reminded of his callousness and lack of love.

"How dare you assume I would be desperate enough to marry a complete stranger?" she asked before turning to Priscilla. "How long have you known about this? Is this why you befriended me?"

Priscilla cast her face down. "I agreed to help him. I cannot say more. Please believe that I have enjoyed our friendship."

"Stop!" Alaina snapped. "Aunt Cornelia was right. She questioned your motives and your unexpected visits, but I thought I'd found a friend."

"I am your friend. I had—"

"That is enough, Priscilla," Harrington interrupted.

Regaining her control, Alaina met Harrington's eyes. "Why should I be shocked? My father's underhanded ways should not surprise me." She pointed to the document he held. "And when did you and my father decide to plan my future?"

Harrington refolded the paper and placed it in his coat pocket and sat down. "Your father and I were in the midst of discussing my compensation for our business arrangement in America when I saw you. You had just attended your mother who was seriously ill as I remember. You came to his study to deliver a message to him. I remember he was quite irritated at you for interrupting. I was party to the rather abrupt communication."

"And I became the subject of your conversation," she said with no attempt to hide her bitterness.

Harrington continued. "I couldn't help but

notice your beauty and vibrancy even at such a young age. I told your father just that. You were perhaps fifteen at the time and obviously unaware of my reaction to you. Your father seemed pleased. The agreement was made."

"I was thrown in to seal a *bargain*?"

"I prefer not to see it as coarsely as you suggest, Miss Craymore. Your father, I am certain, was looking out for your best interests. I am a man of some means and our partnership seemed certain to increase my prestige."

"My interests were never his concern, and I assure you, Mr. Harrington, I am perfectly capable of deciding my own future. Perhaps you might tell me why you have chosen to come and present me with this useless information after all this time."

Harrington's lip curled as he met her glare. Alaina observed the tightness about his mouth that she'd noticed earlier. She waited, sensing the change in his mood. He stared at her for a moment without speaking. His eyes appeared to darken.

"Miss Craymore," Harrington said quietly. "I had a faint hope that you might possibly entertain the idea of marriage, considering your age. It would have made things easier. I even wished that I could have moved more slowly, perhaps been able to take the time to persuade you of the advantages. After all, I am not unpleasant-looking and am sufficiently able to support you." Without warning, his voice took on a sharper edge. "However, I haven't the time to waste on an extended courtship."

"Then the matter is settled," Alaina said,

squaring her shoulders.

"The matter of the betrothal for the time being, perhaps, but we have other matters to discuss that you might take more seriously." Harrington leaned forward and clasped his hands together.

Alaina hadn't noticed how tightly she was gripping the arms of her chair until she forced herself to stand. "I believe it is time for you both to leave. Our business is done." Before she could call Thomas to see him out, Harrington stood and grasped her arm.

Alaina shrugged back from his touch.

"Miss Craymore, I suggest that you hear me out. You might want to sit back down."

Alaina drew back at the warning note in his voice. Before more could be said, a servant tapped at the open door.

"Miss Alaina, I apologize for the interruption but could I have a few minutes of your time? We have a problem in the kitchen. I wouldn't bother you while you have guests but Lady Henley isn't home and Cook is in a frenzy."

"I'll be right there, Edith." She turned to her visitors. "I believe we are done here."

"Please, attend to your housekeeper's problem," Harrington said, returning to his seat. "We'll wait until you return."

Alaina stiffened her jaw. She wanted both him and Priscilla gone, but she didn't want to rouse Edith's concern. She followed Edith out the door, wondering what more could be said that would make her day any worse.

HARRINGTON HAD observed Richard Craymore for a week before visiting his townhouse. He wanted to get the measure of the man he'd hoped would be willing to represent his father's interests. Instead Craymore agreed to only a brief introduction, telling him to leave the papers he needed to discuss with him, to his butler. He was too busy preparing to leave on a business trip, Harrington mused, as he watched Alaina leave with the servant. He'd left London without a word, though he'd left the address of his hotel with his servant. He most likely hadn't even glanced at the documents he'd left behind to his detriment. Miss Craymore could not refuse.

The Chinese businessmen who he and Lord Craymore had wooed for months before his death were ready to sign a trade deal that would make Harrington among the wealthiest men in Boston. He was not going to let Craymore's death stand in the way of completing the transaction.

The men traveled twice a year from China to America and back so Craymore's death went without notice. Only recently, when he had completed most aspects of the trade agreement had they asked for Lord Craymore to be present at the signing. Despite the language barriers, the men were shrewd and inflexible. Having done business with British traders in the past, they trusted a lord of the realm more than Harrington, a Boston businessman with few credentials to his credit. Yet it was he that had done most of the groundwork over the past year, while Craymore lay in his grave.

He turned to Priscilla. "Stop shrinking into the

fabric of that settee. You look like a frightened mouse. You know what I expect of you. You must help me convince Miss Craymore to travel to America with me. If not, you know the consequences."

"She does not deserve this."

"If her brother had been more like his father, I would not have involved her."

"And if I had not been fooled by your friendly façade when we first met, I wouldn't be a party to your scheme."

"True, but you have little choice in the matter now, unless you care to defy me."

Priscilla's shoulders shuddered. She looked away.

He smirked. He'd created the desire effect.

He turned his back to her and reviewed the entire situation in his mind to be sure he hadn't missed anything. Lord Craymore had believed that trade between China and America was a great avenue of wealth, especially since the elite Bostonians desired the tea, porcelain, silks and coarse cottons from China that had been imported to Britain for years. With America's new freedoms fought for in the Revolutionary War, businessmen were able to take advantage of the lucrative market, but in decades since, they had done little. The Chinese expected to have trade go both ways. America had little to offer them. Lord Craymore wasn't one to ignore profits, even if they needed be gotten through underhanded means. He knew the Chinese had a taste for opium and Turkish markets were ready to do business.

Harrington had spent the year firming up agreements and courting Boston businessmen who could back his endeavors, and all after Craymore had died. His reputation would be in shreds if he couldn't keep the beneficial promises he'd made to them.

He also hoped to bring an end to his other business, one he had to admit, he enjoyed, but of late it had become more difficult to stay in the shadows, despite his alias. If it were found out that he was involved in the disreputable enterprise, he would become a pariah to the purists in Boston.

He'd already wasted close to three months figuring out a plan, which included this trip to England. He had to be on the next ship out of Liverpool. Once he arrived back in Boston, he would have only a few weeks to complete the deal. If the Chinese representatives become dissatisfied with his efforts and give the contract to someone else, all he'd worked for would be lost. It wasn't going to happen.

Telling them of his betrothal to Craymore's daughter was genius. He'd immediately seen that they were impressed that a British lord would think so highly of him as to let him marry his daughter. Regardless, they wanted proof of Craymore's continued involvement.

Richard Craymore would have been the perfect substitute but he'd refused to take the time to listen to his offer. His other business took on more importance — imprudent man. Alaina, Craymore's loving daughter and his devoted fiancée, must be the convincing factor. Even that might not be enough. If she could convince them that her father was ill but dedicated to the project and thought enough of closing the deal to send his own daughter in his stead, it might suffice. It was a last-ditch effort but if in the end they signed the contract, it was worth dragging her to America.

Gaining her participation was the most difficult obstacle he'd had to overcome. He should have made a point to become better acquainted with her sooner, He'd hoped she'd be ripe to seduce. In his investigations into the Craymore scandal and the gossip surrounding it, he'd learned that her reputation was in most respects ruined in proper society due to her father's deeds. No suitors were knocking at her door. To his disappointment, the news of the betrothal infuriated her.

Her devotion to her brother was his next card. He was gambling on her love and loyalty to him.

"Phillip."

Priscilla drew his attention. He frowned when he looked her way. She appeared to still be cowering on the couch.

"Phillip, is there no other option? I fear Alaina will refuse to go with you or she might tell Lady Henley. Your plan could go entirely wrong."

He didn't miss the desperation in her voice. He took the few steps toward her, leaned down until his face was a few inches from hers. "You befriended her, gained her confidence. It was you who told me how much she adores her brother, looks up to him. I trust your information is accurate. If she refuses me, then you must use your wiles to convince her to be on that ship to

America."

"I said I would try. That must be enough," she whispered.

"Trying is not enough," he said. "You will succeed or find another way to pay your creditors." He leered at her, noting as he had in the past, her curvaceous figure. He stood and strode away from her, leaving her to think of her own dire situation and what she needed to do to overcome it.

It had taken some time on his last visit to encourage her to befriend Alaina. He knew what persuasive tactics to use for each unique situation. In fact, he was a genius at his work. Priscilla was sliding swiftly into debt by her own admission and hounded by creditors who were demanding more than money. He had promised her generous compensation and protection. He smirked at the thought of her vulnerability. Once he left for Boston with Alaina, he would be done with her.

The door opened and Alaina walked in, looking agitated. She shut the door firmly behind her, but took only a few steps into the room. "Mr. Harrington, you say you have another issue to discuss with me. Please get it over with. I want both of you gone from my sight as soon as possible."

Miss Craymore was behaving like a termagant. It was time to end this charade of courtesy. She was getting under his skin with her defiance and he needed her under his thumb. "The matter is of great importance and I must have your assistance."

"What could you possible want from me?"

He paused before answering, clasping his

hands together. "Your immediate and congenial cooperation to travel to America as my fiancée and, obviously, your name, Miss Craymore."

Harrington's pronouncement received the effect he'd hoped for. Her mouth dropped open as she took an abrupt step back.

"You must be insane. First, you present me with a betrothal of which I had no knowledge, and now you want me to go to America with you? Please leave." She reached for the door handle.

"The matter concerns your brother's freedom, his very life." His lips turned up in a sneering grin. He'd gotten her attention. He reached into the pocket of his topcoat and pulled out the documents he'd purposely held until the last. He held them out to her. "I am sorry to have to do this. If I had any other recourse..."

"I believe your contriteness to be as false as whatever papers you hold in your hand."

"Decide for yourself." He shrugged as he placed them in her outstretched hand. As she scanned the papers, he gauged her reaction. She seemed to be trying her best to hide her emotions but she wasn't fooling him. Her face grew pale and her chin trembled as she studied them.

"Where did you get these?" Alaina demanded.

"Your father enjoyed bragging about his escapades, particularly when we sat and enjoyed the excellent brandy he procured without having to pay revenue to customs. He told me how the system worked, barrels of fine liquor sunk off shore and at night retrieved and placed in caves away from the eyes of collectors of revenue. Of course, alcohol was only one type of contraband. Your father had no scruples when it came to possessing items of value that could be imported without customs handling."

"You and my father were involved in smuggling too?"

"Notice that my name is not on those documents. Your father liked to boast of his gains. Because I felt the need to have security over my investment of time and labor, I found it quite easy to pocket some of the papers he enjoyed flaunting, just in case he conveniently forgot to pay me for my services. One must never be too trusting, you know. I couldn't help but notice when I perused them at my leisure that your brother's signature appeared on many of them. Your father, of course, has escaped prosecution. Death is sometimes convenient. Your brother, on the other hand, I understand is doing fairly well at this time, trying to overcome the blackness of your name, that is according to your friend Priscilla who you have so conveniently confided in." Harrington nodded toward the couch where Priscilla sat.

Priscilla looked away.

"Perhaps if you possessed some papers with your brother's signature, Miss Craymore, you would see that these not only hold the proof that your brother trafficked in uncustomed goods but that he took part in bribing customs officials to overlook contraband."

"I *know* my brother's signature."

"Then you must see the obvious."

He saw her body shudder. *Good.*

"If these papers were to get into the hands of the authorities," he continued, "they'd present more than enough proof of your brother's criminal involvement in a sophisticated smuggling operation, punishable by imprisonment or even death."

"Richard is not a smuggler," Alaina said between clenched teeth. She glared at Priscilla. "You knew of these accusations?"

Priscilla nodded, looking ashamed. "I respect your brother, Alaina. You have told me how hard he's worked to reestablish himself and regain his reputation. When Phillip showed me these papers, I had to hear him out. I feel wretched over this."

"You have no conscience," Alaina snapped. "I trusted you."

Harrington sighed. He had no time for women's emotional outbursts. "Your brother signed these receipts and bills of lading. I preferred not to be involved in your father's more covert affairs, though he urged me to take advantage of opportunities. My only concern was our collaboration on a trade agreement with China that promises to make me a very wealthy man. Unfortunately your father died before it was finished. I continued to work toward procuring the agreement, obviously without your father's aid, though I had no choice but to use his name and reputation. Now my interests are in jeopardy unless I can demonstrate your father's continued commitment."

"I care nothing for your interests, Mr. Harrington, and my father is dead."

"Be that as it may, the men are not aware of your father's passing. I tried to contact your brother. Rather than taking the time to examine the evidence, he left London and is now unreachable."

"He is out of town on business. He won't return for weeks."

"And I cannot wait. I've been given a deadline I must adhere to or lose a fortune. My associates are impatient. The voyage back to America will take a month. That leaves me, perhaps, two weeks, maybe three to meet their deadline once I return. I need to be on the next ship leaving Liverpool and have a Craymore in attendance as your father's representative. You are the only one available. I need you to accompany me as my fiancée, with a chaperone, of course."

"I cannot just pack up and leave. What would I tell Lady Henley? My reputation as frail as it is would be beyond repair." She shook her head. "No! You must realize what you are demanding is unconscionable."

"Miss Craymore, perhaps I have not made myself clear. If you don't agree to help me, these papers will be in the hands of the police before I board ship. Do you understand?" He took a step closer, forcing her to step back. "I am not culpable for your brother's illegal activities. If I go back to Boston alone, these papers go to the authorities and your brother will be arrested immediately upon his return to London."

"My brother...you must understand." She lowered her eyes and folded her hands to her lips.

Harrington observed her confusion and

obvious fright. He was pleased that he had succeeded in breaking through her protective wall. "Of course, if you have little regard for your brother and choose your reputation over his ruination then I will leave immediately."

"You do not know my brother! A father carries great influence on a son. Richard sought to please him. He worked by his side." She looked away, murmuring more to herself than to her audience. "He was very young, ambitious. He could have signed papers without the knowledge of what they contained. He came to realize my father's deceitful nature. He distanced himself, refusing to be party to his unscrupulous activities."

"That is all well and good, my dear. We often regret our past actions. However, the damage was done. Being a party to smuggling carries severe penalties. I doubt that you want to see your brother imprisoned." He stopped and rubbed his chin. "Or his swollen body tied to London docks, though that practice, I believe, has been discontinued. Imprisonment or banishment is enough to destroy any man."

Alaina's hand went to her throat. Priscilla rushed to her side and tried to reach out to her. Harrington held Priscilla back. A bit more coaxing and he would have his way.

"You must calm yourself, Miss Craymore. I have become desperate myself. Otherwise I would not resort to such measures. I am in business to make profits. I have tried to handle the situation civilly, but have gotten nowhere. I can wait no longer. I must leave tomorrow evening for

Liverpool. *If* you involve anyone else, these papers go immediately to the authorities before I board the ship. I understand that you no longer hold a place in society of any true value. Sad state of affairs and, no doubt, your status is undeserving. If we marry, the Harrington name will erase your stigma of being a Craymore. You can reestablish yourself as the wife of a wealthy man."

"I would never marry you, nor will I believe that my brother is a criminal. He couldn't have known what he was signing."

"Without question, bacon-brained freebooters are hired to do the dirty work, but that does not exonerate your brother, as you must realize. These papers prove his involvement."

"And you would blackmail me into cooperating?"

He gave her a tight-lipped grin. "Unfortunately, I am left with no other choice. I do not resort to violence to obtain what I want. I am a businessman and negotiator by nature. Information used to the best advantage, I believe, holds more force than a fist and is far less messy. Once the agreement is signed, you can return to England on the next ship. Though you may change your mind about leaving. You might prefer the hospitality of Americans over the stuffiness of the English."

He straightened his waistcoat and flicked off a tiny piece of lint from a sleeve. "A coach has been hired for tomorrow evening and a chaperone acquired to accompany you. Priscilla will help you with your travel needs and inform you of my arrangements. I recommend that you accept her assistance since no one else can be told of the reasons for your departure."

"Please, I cannot leave Mrs. Henley without a word."

"If that is your position, I have no alternative than to visit the police immediately." He pulled the papers from Alaina's hand and tucked them into a coat pocket. "Your brother's arrest and imprisonment will rest on your conscience." He turned to leave.

"No! If you would only wait until my brother returns. I beg you, he will straighten everything out."

"And all I've worked for will be lost." He buttoned his coat. "Priscilla, are you coming?"

"Alaina, please reconsider," Priscilla pleaded. "Phillip promised me you need only to play a part for a short time. You would come to no harm and can return once these contracts he talks of are signed. I know how much your brother means to you." She brushed tears from her eyes. "I care about him too. I realize you may feel that your reputation would be beyond repair, but I will help you in any way I can. Richard's *life* is at stake. You mustn't let Phillip do this. My betrayal may be unforgiveable, but he will follow through with his threat and Richard will suffer for it."

Alaina crossed her arms tightly about her as if the room had suddenly grown cold. Harrington watched, unmoving, waiting.

"Think of your brother imprisoned," Priscilla pleaded. "Your reputation in society will mean nothing with your brother locked in a cell."

Alaina looked at Priscilla before nodding, her lips trembling, her expression resigned.

Harrington drew in a breath, concealing his relief.

"You are wise, Miss Craymore. You will need traveling clothes, especially warmer wraps for the ship voyage and sturdy shoes or boots. Priscilla will return tomorrow afternoon and help you to gather what I suggest. Tomorrow at midnight, I will wait in a carriage up the street." He pointed in the direction of where he would be. "I expect that you will be on time. Your chaperone will be with me. When we arrive in Boston, we will shop and add to your wardrobe."

"I don't want her help." She glared at Priscilla. "I want nothing from either of you."

"And how do you plan to pack a trunk under the eyes of your benefactor and her servants and carry it out in the middle of the night?" Harrington goaded. "You must be sensible. I will instruct Priscilla on the most useful items. You can determine how best to transfer items to her carriage without notice during her visit."

"Lady Henley attends her sewing circle on Thursday afternoon, if I recall," Priscilla said. "I'll come while she's gone. We are of similar size, I'll add some of my own gowns later in a trunk to be brought to the ship. Alaina, please accept my help. Your sacrifice is noble."

"Get out of my sight," Alaina muttered, turning away.

"I'll arrive at two and help…"

Harrington waved a hand for Priscilla to say no

more and follow him out the door. He ignored the tears streaming down her face. Enough of women's hysterics. He had nothing else to say to Miss Craymore whose back was turned to him.

He sneered, aware that sometimes silence spoke louder than a final word.

ALAINA SAT on her bed, tears dried. She'd barely moved a muscle over the past few hours. Harrington's revelations and threats, Priscilla's betrayal, her father's visit from the grave—at least that's what it felt like—had swept her into a storm tide of rage and disbelief. She'd finally regained some control. It was time to prepare for what she must do.

She would leave letters for Aunt Cornelia, Richard and Marielle, her dearest friend. She would tell them of her surprise when she heard of the betrothal and her decision to accept, and that her fiancé, a successful businessman, had to return to America posthaste. The letters would appear shallow and her decision rash. They were aware of her despondency over the past year. Perhaps they would see her leaving as an avenue of escape from society's treatment of her since her father's death or, more likely, that she'd snapped and lost her mind. There was nothing else she could say to ease their thoughts.

She exhaled a tortured breath as some of the horrors of the past hour returned. What if he wanted more than just her presence? What if he expected her to marry him, or ruin her in other ways? What if she didn't survive the crossing to

America? She'd never been on a ship and she'd heard of deaths on long journeys. She shook her head. These thoughts had held her prisoner for the past few hours. She had to block them out, go forward, or witness her brother's ruination.

But how could she just walk out the door, perhaps never return? Leaving meant tossing aside the possibility that society would accept her someday as someone other than her father's daughter. It meant giving up the dreams of Martin returning and wanting to be with her. In her secret heart, she'd yearned to see him again, had held out hope that he would return to her and they could heal from the past together.

She pressed her hands to her temples. She wanted to scream but everyone was asleep and unaware of what she was going through. She'd pretended all was fine, that she had a headache and wanted to go to bed early. Fortunately, Aunt Cornelia had been tired from her day's activities and had retired after dinner.

She went to her writing desk, thinking about what she could possibly say to ease the shock of those she would leave behind. *If I could only wake up from this nightmare. If there was another way.* Her gaze fell on an unopened letter on the desk. Edith must have placed it there earlier. Her visit with Harrington and Priscilla had distracted her from ordinary events of the day.

"Oh *God*," she breathed, realizing it was a letter from her brother. She broke the seal, her heart pounding as she unfolded his letter, holding out the smallest hope that an answer might be enclosed. Her brother had saved her from grief so often. *I need your help more than ever, Richard.* She read, each word causing a deeper ache in her heart.

My dearest Alaina,

I hope this finds you well, though the news I am about to disclose may jar your spirit and cause you immeasurable anguish. Regrettably, I must prepare you for impending events. An unexpected visitor brought documents that I ignored in my anxiety to leave for my appointment in Chelsea. I took them with me to read on my route from London. The information contained has caused much despair and, I fear, implications beyond my power to ignore. I prefer not to go into the details in a letter, for what I must tell you will be disheartening enough. I know no other way to break the news, my dear sister.

When my business is done and I return to London, I expect that the authorities will be at my door with a warrant for my arrest. Information of a criminal nature will be in their hands by then. The evidence they hold will be difficult if not impossible for me to explain away. Therefore it is a certainty that I will be detained and possibly imprisoned. I have no idea what the eventual outcome will be, though I will do my best to prove my ignorance of the charges. My concerns have been and always will be for your well-being and in a matter of weeks you will be forced to face another scandal. I send my deepest regrets for having to forewarn you, but I feel I must. I pray that God will be your protector during the months ahead, and you will eventually be freed from the dishonor you have been forced to bear.

With sincere devotion,
Richard

She crushed the letter to her breast. *Richard knows of the charges and takes them seriously, enough to expect arrest.* She could no longer hope that Harrington's proof had no basis or that her brother would be saved from the accusations.

She could not allow him to face the humiliation, the disgrace, and worse, the imprisonment that would surely follow. She had no doubt that Harrington would carry out his threat. She'd recognized her brother's signature, implicating him in crimes against the Crown. Richard spoke of ignorance, which meant it was true. He'd most likely signed papers without full knowledge of their contents. She had to believe that. How could he possibly prove innocence?

I'll not let him rot in prison as Lord Blackstone did. Never! She thought of the times her brother protected her from their father's wrath. Now she could protect him. She could not choose her own life over his. Priscilla had been right. She could not choose her position in society over her brother's imprisonment.

She had to accept Priscilla's aid in her flight from London, despite her betrayal. She believed Priscilla when she said she cared for her brother and feared for what Harrington might do. It was obvious that she was distraught over the entire situation. Still, she could never forgive her. She'd confided in her, shared stories of her and Richard's lives under her father's dominance. She'd believed she'd truly found a friend amidst society's rejection. Instead Priscilla had planned their meeting, had worked with Harrington while pretending to be a trusted friend. Aunt Cornelia had always been suspicious of her friendship and had tried to caution her. The sweet old woman had wisdom and foresight that Alaina lacked.

She cringed as she considered the future in a land she knew little of and with a man she knew even less about, only that he, like her father, chose wealth over virtue. Yet how different could it be? *After all, I've lived most of my life under the rule of a tyrant.*

GRATEFUL THAT the house was quiet, Alaina closed the front door quietly behind her the next night, holding only a small satchel in her gloved hands. A dark, hooded cloak covered her dull, gray traveling dress. She faced the darkness, misty enough to hide stars, and fled down the stairs to the sidewalk, stopping for only a moment to look back at what had been her safe haven.

She could not allow sentiment or a doubt to return. She had to remain as she'd been since Priscilla had left, numbed, hollow, as if she was moving forward in a trance.

Looking around to be sure no one was about, she rushed up the street. Harrington stood by the carriage, dressed in black. Though he grinned when she approached, she saw only menace.

"You are punctual, my dear."

He offered his arm to help her into the carriage. She pushed it away and climbed in to find a girl younger than her sitting there. Harrington climbed in after her and knocked on the roof. The carriage moved forward.

"Miss Craymore, allow me to introduce Molly Krimps. She will be your maid and companion."

"*She* is to be my chaperone?"

"Molly's father was pleased to offer his daughter's services. He is a poor tradesman with many children. I promised to find Molly a position in America so she could send home wages that will help the family."

"She is no more than a child." Alaina wanted to grab the handle of the door and jump from the carriage. If she died, all this would end. No more thinking, sacrificing, fearing all that was ahead of her. She pushed the dire thoughts away when she realized the girl was speaking to her.

"I'm eighteen, though I look young for my age, Mr. Harrington 'ere is going to find me a well-payin' position. Ain't nothin' 'ere for me to do but get Papa mad. Says I'm eatin' his food without contributin'. Never been a maid, but I'll do my best to please you, Miss." Molly smiled, a broken tooth marring what appeared to be a pretty face in the darkness of the carriage.

The girl's chatting helped to ease Alaina's terror. She breathed in deeply, swallowed down her fear. From the few words spoken, Alaina could tell the girl had little education, if any, and that her father was glad to be rid of her. At least she would not be alone with Harrington.

The girl appeared excited to go to America and chatted on without seeming to notice the tension in the carriage. After they'd traveled a few miles, the girl nodded off to sleep, her head resting on

Alaina's shoulder.

Alaina stared out into the darkness, refusing to speak to Harrington. He'd made only one attempt to converse with her, asking her to call him Phillip and addressing her by her given name. She'd refused to answer him. Her silence didn't seem to make a difference to him. He appeared deep in thought, while the paralyzing sense of foreboding and the indecency of her actions weighed on her and kept her wide awake and watchful.

The next few days were a blur. True to his promise, Phillip made no other demands. When they stopped at inns on their way to the Liverpool docks, Alaina and Molly shared a room and were roused early to continue their journey. As they came closer to their destination, they traveled through the night in order to arrive at the docks before dawn. Conversation took place only when necessary. They arrived none too soon. The ship was loading the last of its cargo and passengers were standing about ready to board.

At the last moment, Molly pushed ahead through the crowd. Alaina watched her youthful companion disappear, her excitement at boarding taking precedence over her assignment. Alaina backed away, fear taking hold. The massive ship, the swarm of bodies, the smells of sweat and salt overcame her senses. She needed to escape.

"I can't do this," she mumbled. If she boarded, it would be the end of all she held dear, the broken strands left of her reputation, the people she loved, the life she knew.

"Please, Phillip," she thrust his given name

from her lips. "Please don't do this. I can't…"

"But you will." Harrington remained calm, obviously prepared for her resistance. He flashed papers in front of her, sealed and ready to hand to the dock master. Her breath caught. She stared at the package of documents.

She boarded without a word.

Chapter Two
Aboard ship, late March

THE TRUTH, not the harsh wind, caused Alaina to shiver as the ship prepared to sail. She turned her back to the waves beating harshly against the ship's side and glared at the man she was forced to call her fiancé. He expected a congenial tone in her voice in the presence of others. She complied by speaking only when spoken to. She cared little if those on board thought she might be dull-witted. Harrington had no problem carrying a conversation himself. She abhorred the arrogance in his tone as he boasted to another passenger of the success he'd achieved in America.

She thought of Martin who had taken the same journey for adventure. Living among high society now that his father's name was cleared had brought him no satisfaction. She knew that much about him. He'd lived too many years on the streets, trying to survive after his family was forced off their estate. What excitement he must have felt standing where she was right now, watching the ocean waves batter the ship's sides. So different from the darkness she felt in her heart.

"No wonder he left for America," she murmured as the cap she wore loosened in the wind. She tied the ribbon more securely under her chin and drew in a ragged breath. If he'd stayed, even if their relationship had gone further, she would always be a reminder of his family's suffering.

Regardless, her dreams were shattered by her present reality. How ironic to be on her way toward the man she loved, while being in the presence of a man she despised. If there was even a remote possibility that she might cross Martin's path, she could only turn away in shame. She'd left London with a man she didn't even know and agreed to pose as his intended. Her actions, regardless of her reasons, would place her in a permanent state of disgrace. How could she ever return? She would be banished from decent society.

Now, as she watched the black waves slap at the side of the ship, she thought it seemed appropriate that they were leaving on a rough sea.

Wiping unwanted tears, she promised herself that she would not allow weakness to overtake her again. She focused on the sailors walking around the capstan. She watched as they pushed at the bars, their gruff voices filling the cold, damp air with a hardy song. She blocked her anxious thoughts and joined the other passengers to watch and listen.

Way, hay, up she rises,
Way, hay, up she rises,
Earlye in the morning.

The sailors stamped their feet on the deck as they pushed, chanting the chorus while passengers either sang along with the crew or leaned over railings to wave their final goodbye to loved ones gathered on the dock. The cacophony of sounds mixed with the smells of the sea created an atmosphere so overwhelming she found herself immersed in the newness, afraid, exhilarated, awed, all her senses alert—aware that she was leaving all that she loved, perhaps for the last time. For Martin, he must have faced the adventure of a lifetime. To her, it was the end of all she held dear. Her thoughts reeled as she held more tightly to the railing while the boat rocked and the chanting and stamping continued.

Way, hay, up she rises,
Way, hay, up she rises,
Earlye in the morning.

As sailors hoisted the sails and hauled the sheets to windward, she listened to the talk of the passengers around her. While they spoke of the packet ships which had been completing voyages once a month from Liverpool to New York since as early as 1818, crew members warned them to be open to the unexpected, for the weather was the true determiner of their fate.

Once the ship was underway, Alaina became absorbed in watching the crew going about their duties. When night came, she found it difficult to sleep but as the days passed, she became accustomed to the noises and swaying of the vessel, even the occasional rowdiness of a passenger or member of the crew. Molly became seasick a day out of port and spent most of the time in the stateroom they shared. The ship's physician gave her medicine that did little to ease her discomfort but did help her to sleep a good part of the time. Thankfully, Phillip left her mostly to herself as he caroused with other passengers. Though he introduced her as his fiancée, thankfully, he demanded nothing from her.

She became accustomed to the consistent schedule kept onboard as well as the songs the sailors sang as they worked. Different tunes were sung depending on the job at the time, ones for raising or lowering the sails and others when they had a brief time to rest. She consumed only enough to keep up her strength, while other passengers spent most of each day eating and drinking.

During the day, she walked on deck and allowed the salt air and the wind to lift her spirits. Occasionally Molly walked with her, but more often, when she felt well enough, she'd be playing cards with one of the young shipmates. Alaina thought of Martin often. She carried his letter and his Boston address, but the dim hope that he could help her was erased by the reality of her disreputable actions.

She couldn't deny her own moments of awe at being in the middle of the ocean without seeing land or even another ship. Nights were especially fascinating and frightening. She'd stare out at the blackness and except for stars on a clear night, it seemed as if nothing else existed but this one ship in an immense universe. It was those times she felt most alone.

Thankfully, Phillip made no attempt to take advantage of her virtue. He wanted nothing to affect her posturing in the presence of others. As the days passed, she gained a sense of his need to project an air of dignity and refinement. She wondered if he'd demand more from her when they reached America. When those disturbing thoughts crowded in, she did her best to block them out.

They had been on the ocean for twenty-three days and they were nearing the end of their voyage when a stormy night proved to be the worst of all. At times, she feared being swept overboard, at other moments, drowning seemed more favorable than spending her life with Phillip Harrington.

"Come, Alaina. We'll both catch a chill in this blasted wind," Harrington said loudly as he came to her side. His words were slurred from drinking most of the evening. The captain who had been barking orders to his hands on deck, walked toward them, his fingers pointing to the hold, obviously urging them to go below.

"Perhaps the good captain will have one of his men bring us some warm brandy to weather the storm."

The captain, busy inspecting a line, appeared stunned by Harrington's request, his harsh response was nearly swallowed by the noise of billowing sails and creaking ropes. "In due time. At the moment my men are busy keeping this ship on course and stable."

Alaina scowled at Phillip. "I am in no need of brandy. The captain has enough to think about without catering to us."

"Come," he snapped. "The cold and dampness

will settle in those lovely bones."

He stood too close, his hand on her arm. She recoiled from his touch, stumbling on the wet planks. He caught her and held her firmly.

"I do not require your assistance," she muttered through clenched teeth as she struggled to keep her balance, nearly falling on top of a large, wooden chest.

"Without it you will be swabbing the deck with your wrap from one end to the other." With great reluctance, she allowed him to help her manage the steps to the lower compartments. "Perhaps you might consider joining me in my cabin for that brandy?"

"I prefer to retire."

"Since we've left England, I have catered to your desires. You must admit I have been a gentleman. I haven't behaved in an unseemly manner and your virtue is still intact." He smirked. "You behave as if I have broken my promises."

Alaina grasped the handle of her cabin door, fear rising in her at the change in his behavior and the stench of alcohol on his breath. "You promised to allow me my privacy."

"And I will carry out our agreement," he whispered as he grounded himself firmly in front of her, his hands pressed against the boards above her head and his face too close to hers. "After all, I have a reputation to uphold in America."

"A reputation you do not deserve," Alaina cut in, her head turned to the side.

Harrington ignored her retort. "I look forward to introducing my fiancée to my acquaintances. In time, I believe you will enjoy life in America. You may even choose to stay, perhaps even be thankful that I am the one who holds the evidence of your brother's misdeeds. It could be someone who has no scruples. I must admit that I was surprised that with your beauty, you were not already taken." He reached out to brush away a damp curl that rested on her cheek, her skin now raw from the wind.

She slapped away his hand.

Phillip wore an amused grin as she clung to the door handle, unable to push open the door or to keep her balance. "Perhaps the success of the venture may interest your brother. He may want to continue the partnership I had with your father. He might even desire our marriage once he sees the profits. Your reputation would be salvaged. Have you given that some thought?"

"Richard will never become involved in your affairs and we will never marry. This engagement is as deceitful as your scheme," Alaina hissed, as the door opened slightly then slammed shut as the ship swayed. She tugged again with all her strength only to have Phillip twist her shoulders until she faced him. The tightness of the quarters left little room between them.

"Your brother may eventually realize his error in not cooperating, Alaina. Furthermore, seeing your belligerence, he may now appreciate that I have relieved him of his responsibility toward you."

"Please allow me to retire," she pleaded. "Molly was quite ill today. I must see how she is faring."

"Ah, yes, your chaperone," Phillip said. He rubbed her chin with his thumb. "Once the agreement is signed, I will tell the men involved that your father has passed on and you must return to London immediately. You see, Alaina, I am a man of compassion." He bent down and brushed his lips against her forehead, before she could pull away.

Enraged, she gave the door a solid push with her back, forcing it to spring open. He chuckled when she nearly fell through.

Regaining her balance, she slammed the door shut behind her, her body shaking as she stared at her naïve companion sleeping peacefully.

THE APRIL day was dark and dismal though it was barely past two in the afternoon when the ship entered New York harbor. A damp breeze brushed Alaina's face as she stood with other passengers against the ship's rails. She followed the flight of squawking seagulls as they circled smaller sailing vessels, while others skimmed over the water in search of food. Fear and awe filled her senses. Soon she would step on American soil, a land of promise to so many, but to her a place where loneliness and fear would be her companions. How could she feel amazement and terror in the same instant?

Despite her bewilderment, the excitement of the other passengers was contagious. She listened to the chatter of men and women, some of whom were joining family who had arrived earlier. She heard men talk about the progress of a new canal that was to connect the East and West by a continuing waterway. Others were excited about the possibilities of new opportunities in the textile industry or as merchants. Two of the younger men talked about working on whaling ships, jobs they'd read about in letters from family members who had bragged about their success in America. Small children, some who were sick throughout a good part of the voyage, were now clinging to their parents and looking wide-eyed at the sights and sounds about them. Molly stood by a young girl close to her own age that she had met on the journey, both of them pale but smiling.

The passengers had intrigued her throughout the voyage. She'd read that class distinction, so prominent in England, was blurred in this new land, and that newcomers could gain immense wealth and prestige through hard work rather than heredity. Like her, many who were standing near her had never been to America and they too faced an uncertain future. The women especially displayed a nervous excitement, their eyes scanning the land, looking for a familiar face in the crowd of onlookers who waited on the dock. While wives expressed their sadness at leaving loved ones behind, the men onboard were slapping each other on their backs and grinning from ear to ear, fully embracing their new adventure. She found herself fascinated and, for at least a brief time, able to put aside her own grief as she listened to their hopes and dreams. She thought of Martin and wondered what his first reaction was at the sight of the new world.

None of her reading about America had

prepared her for the view before her. Her insides vibrated with trepidation that had little to do with her precarious situation and more to do with the realization that this strange land might be her new home.

She looked through the crowd on the pier, scanning faces, wishing to see Martin while acknowledging the foolishness of such a thought. She wondered if he had already left Boston for other parts of the country, even boarded a ship back to England. That possibility depressed her. She didn't want to admit that in the deepest part of herself, she prayed that their paths might cross.

Time seemed endless as they prepared to disembark. A customs officer boarded the ship and spent a great deal of time inspecting cargo, then more time going over the passenger list. Another hour passed before their baggage was taken off the ship and they could finally step onto dry land.

Her legs felt strange, wobbly and weak. It took some time for her to walk with even steps. Phillip directed her to a quieter dock while he handled the baggage and talked with the captain and the customs officer.

Finding a spot in which to wait, she looked down into the water below. A small rowboat tied to a mooring bobbed as each wave sloshed against the wooden pilings and retreated. The boat, stirred by the breeze, floated like a dream past her, then jerked back, trapped by the rope that held it. Like the boat, she wanted to be released from the bonds that held her in Harrington's grasp.

The dreams she had gathered like flowers after

her father's death were left in England, along with her friends and family. In this alien place, she would be dominated by a man who thought only of himself. She'd be a decoration and a means to his goal.

She watched as the little boat, caught by a forceful wave, hit the side of the dock. The sound shook her from her thoughts. Admittedly, her daydreams seemed to be the only thing that kept her sane and they always returned to Martin. She needed to hold on to the sweet memories of their brief encounters in order to face what was ahead. Otherwise she might turn to stone. She sighed as she heard Phillip's voice behind her.

"Everything is taken care of, Alaina. I have hired a coach to take us to the hotel. We'll rest for a night and begin our travels to Boston in the morning." He reached for her arm.

She tried to pull away but he held her tightly and gave her a scathing look.

"There'll be no more of that," he said sharply. "We're in America now and I am in the public eye. I expect your cooperation and gracious behavior. Do you understand?"

Alaina gritted her teeth and nodded, knowing an argument would only make her situation worse. She looked down at her arm. "You are hurting me."

He released her arm, then offered his own, his tone and facial expression having changed instantly to appropriate public behavior as a couple of passengers passed by. "You may come to love America and even come to like me," he whispered in her ear. She pushed her head aside and stifled a rebuke before accepting his arm as he led her to the hired coach.

As the coach traveled through the New York streets, she became absorbed in the new sights. Men in top hats and women in bonnets and simple walking dresses strolled about. Dogs ran freely while horses and carriages traveled through the narrow, rutted streets. An elderly woman, with only a few teeth, smiled gaily as she sold flowers on a corner. She watched as a well-dressed gentleman tipped his hat to a lady walking by before he turned into a draper's shop. Older men rested on benches, smoking cigars, while mothers scurried by, holding their packages in one hand and their restless children in another.

Phillip pointed out the Park Theatre and told them about the performances he'd seen there. He drew their attention to prominent churches, popular dining places, taverns and favorite walking areas. He pointed out a bank, the first to open in New York. Another sign, he explained, of the growing economy.

They'd traveled a relatively short distance when the coach stopped in front of a hotel. Phillip paid the driver while Alaina looked up at the tall brick building not so unlike a London hotel. She sighed in resignation, feeling like a stranger in this strange city and even worse, a stranger to herself.

Phillip signaled to a young boy who waited outside the hotel door to help the footman with their luggage. Alaina refused to part with the small satchel she carried. As it was, it held only a change of clothes, some personal articles and a few pieces of jewelry. She suspected that her English money was useless here, but she'd heard passengers talk about the value of gold and silver. She hoped that if she became desperate, she could sell the jewelry.

Priscilla had added gowns to her trunk. Alaina hoped they were not her more frivolous ones. Though Phillip announced that he would take her shopping if need be, she wanted no favors from him.

Her wardrobe was the least of her worries.

To her relief, he'd paid for two rooms in the hotel. When he unlocked the door to one of the rooms, she paused before following him in.

Phillip's lips slanted at her hesitation. "I only want to check to see that your room is suitable." He lit a lantern and looked about. "Satisfactory for one night."

Alaina stood rigidly by the door, waiting for him to leave while Molly turned her back to both of them and settled in a chair. It wasn't long after their journey began that Alaina had realized that Molly seemed oblivious to the rancor between her and Harrington. The girl was either tired, sick or in a dream world of imagination most of the time.

"You look frightened, my dear," Harrington said. "I assure you that I have no requests of you. We all need rest and after the drinking I did last night and today, celebrating our arrival, I look forward to a good night's sleep." He stepped through the open door, his hand still on the knob. "We must be up at dawn. A small packet leaves for Boston in the morning and I want us to be on it. If you need anything, I'll be in the next room." He looked at Molly who had curled up on the worn, cushioned chair, her eyes already closing. He shook his head, a distasteful expression crossing his face. "Goodnight, Alaina. Please be sure that girl is punctual in the morning."

When he shut the door behind him, she latched it and breathed a sigh of relief. She looked about the shabby room. Though she held no expectations, she hoped that his residence would be an improvement over the hotel room with its musty smell, dingy rug and dreary furnishings.

She walked over to Molly. Sound asleep, she looked like a child barely out of the schoolroom. Alaina took off her shawl and draped it over her. *Perhaps your naiveté protects you, sweet Molly. What will this new world hold for you?* Alaina feared for the girl's future as much as her own.

She yawned, slipped off her boots and lay down on the bed, choosing not to sleep under the faded bedspread. She missed the swaying of the ship to which she'd become accustomed and even more the presence of other travelers. Now she was alone with a childish companion and a man she feared more than the raging storms that had endangered the voyage. Staring up at the yellowed ceiling, she listened to Molly's breathing and the floorboards creaking in the room above. Anxious imaginings crept into her thoughts and clung like dust. She was desperately afraid of tomorrow, of the unknown, and of her role as Phillip's fiancée.

THE NEXT morning, she woke with a start, remembering where she was and what was ahead.

The dim early-morning light shone through the faded curtains. She jumped from the bed, fearful that she might have overslept, but there had been no pounding on the door. After washing her face with cold water and attempting to comb through her snarled curls, she nudged Molly.

"Time to wake up. We must hurry."

"So early?" Molly rubbed her eyes before they grew large with anticipation. "Can't believe we're 'ere." She stood and stretched, Alaina's shawl falling to the floor.

Alaina swept it up quickly. "Freshen up and we'll see about some breakfast. Hopefully when we arrive in Boston we can have a warm bath and a change of clothes."

Just as Alaina tied her cap, Phillip knocked on the door. She opened it and met his eyes before they lowered to the wrinkled gown she'd slept in. Obviously he wasn't pleased, but he made no comment. Had he expected her to be all primped with ribbons and bows at dawn?

"We'll need to have a quick breakfast and be down at the dock by seven. Are you ready to leave?"

Alaina nodded, picked up her small satchel and along with Molly, who looked half asleep, followed him down the stairs to a small dining room. After hard rolls and coffee, they were on their way.

"Did you sleep well enough, ladies?" Phillip asked as he led her from the hotel to a waiting carriage.

Molly smiled weakly.

"As well as might be expected considering the conditions," Alaina answered.

"I realize they were not what you are accustomed to. I am certain you'll find my home more inviting. Boston is a splendid city with much culture and ever-growing commerce. I believe that you'll be pleasantly surprised."

"Can we be on our way?" Alaina asked, wanting him to stop his false pleasantries.

"You are short on words and long on somberness this morning," he teased with a tight-lipped grin. "I suggest that you see this as a new and wondrous adventure, rather than a punishment."

Alaina shrugged as Phillip helped them into the carriage.

THE BOAT trip to Boston was long and far from pleasant. The packet turned out to be a fishing boat with more cargo than passengers and carried a stench of fish. She didn't appreciate the captain leering at them or the foul language used by his crew. Molly wrapped her arm about Alaina's and seemed to shrivel up beside her. Occasionally Phillip checked on them, but Alaina refused to respond to his queries.

Hours later, the boat arrived in Boston harbor. As the boat came into port, the sun began its descent in a beautiful array of color that was mirrored in the water. The pinks and purples that played on the water as well as the vividness of color on the horizon, Alaina had to admit, was beyond beautiful. It was magical.

She decided that she'd do her best to live in the moment and avoid cleaving to the past. She even tried to carry on a civilized conversation with Phillip as they waited to disembark. The sooner she could play her part, the sooner she'd be rid of him and Richard would be out of danger. She wouldn't dwell on her own future. She couldn't.

When they arrived at port, Phillip hired a coach and spent a few minutes talking to the driver while the ladies waited with the luggage. Alaina saw him hand the coachman money before he called Molly over to him and told her to bring her satchel. She complied, and after he said a few words to Molly, she was helped into the carriage. Alaina picked up her own satchel and walked toward them, only to have Phillip wave the carriage off.

Alaina ran toward him as the coach drove away. "Where is Molly going?" she screamed when she reached him. "You've sent her off."

"Alaina, you must not upset yourself. As I told you earlier, Molly's father expects her to send money home to the family. She has a position and she is on her way there now."

"But she is my companion. You told me—"

"She has accompanied you on the journey. Now you must fulfill our bargain. The girl will only be in the way. When we reach my home, you will see that my servants will cater to your needs." Phillip turned away and waved down a coach.

Alaina sucked in a shaky breath at another unexpected change. True, Molly was childish and dependent rather than helpful, but Alaina realized that her presence had been a comfort. At times her concern for the girl's welfare kept her from her own dismal thoughts. Would Molly be safe and secure in her new position? And what was it? Phillip had avoided any discussion of the girl's future.

When the coachman opened the door, Alaina climbed in without another word and stared straight ahead. Arguing was of no use. She clung to her satchel and wondered what other surprises would be in store for her.

Chapter Three

"I AGREE, he is a grand piece of horseflesh," Martin Blackstone said as he admired the large chestnut stallion being paraded in front of him.

"He's a beautiful stepper, comes straight from Kentucky. You won't find a better saddle breed around here for show or riding," the man who held the reins replied. "You won't be disappointed with this one."

Martin admired the horse's sleek neck and fine proportions. The idea of starting a ranch and breeding horses, perhaps some race winners, intrigued him. This horse was the first of many he hoped to purchase.

Once they settled on a price, he took over the reins and led the horse away, but not before letting the man know that he'd be interested in others of the same quality. He decided to walk the horse to the stable he had rented rather than ride. It was a beautiful sunny morning. A spring breeze rustled the trees along the road and few people were about.

As he walked along, keeping the horse at a steady pace, he reflected on the past few weeks. His time in Boston had been exhilarating. He'd met interesting people, played some tough games of cards, won more than he'd lost and now he was ready to move on. Despite his desire to see more of America, he planned to return to England in a few weeks. Thankfully, he'd found a keen-sighted overseer for his newly purchased property in Virginia. He would need to transport this beauty there before he left, he thought, as he patted the horse's mane.

He wanted to see York and Marielle's firstborn, as well as discuss his plans with his brother, perhaps entice them into a visit. Most of all, he needed to see Alaina. He wanted to slide his fingers through her thick mahogany curls as he had done their final night together. He imagined removing those frilly caps or foolish hair combs she often wore, allowing her waves to fall over her creamy, bare shoulders. He'd dreamed too many nights of her and what he wanted from her and what he wanted to give. He still remembered too well the feel of her body when he'd held her in his arms and her brown eyes that deepened with desire after he'd kissed her. The sweet essence of lavender permeated his dreams and caused the frustrating surge of desire to build in his loins. He had to see her, and if she felt the same as he did, convince her to come to America with him.

I must return soon, he thought as he curled his fingers around strands of the horse's mane. He had written her another letter but received no answer. Perhaps it never arrived. Even with the regular schedule of packet ships leaving port for England, it held no guarantee that his letters would be delivered.

He refused to acknowledge his deepest fear. He was a reminder of all she had gone through when their families had been embroiled in scandal. He had wanted her father dead, punished for his deeds against his family. She might want to begin anew, find someone who wouldn't be a constant reminder of the scandal and of her own horrors of that night her father died. Hadn't he thought the same?

Yet he couldn't let her go.

Cornelia Henley and his sister-in-law Marielle were most likely encouraging her to attend the many balls and parties of the Season now that her mourning period was over. Society could be cruel to aristocratic families that had fallen from grace, but Alaina was too beautiful to be left on the shelf.

He hoped that she'd be there waiting...if she hadn't found another. That thought aroused possessive anger. He'd spent too many nights wondering if he had made a mistake leaving so soon after her father's death. He'd convinced himself that she needed time to heal and his presence, as well as his lust—which he'd found almost impossible to stifle in her presence—created an obstacle. But since he'd been away he had realized there was more to his decision to leave.

He needed to find answers, to find out where he belonged. His life had been a maze of confusing roads. Too many years had been spent surviving in a world that had been unknown to him before his father's imprisonment. He'd been a child protected by loving parents and a secure life of wealth and privilege. Their estate was graced with visitors of the highest station. His mother had filled their home with love and beauty—until everything changed because of a jealous, self-seeking tyrant— Alaina's father. Like dominoes, their secure world had tumbled. The thought of the monster caused a bitter taste in Martin's mouth. He spat on the ground and brushed his forearm across his lips.

He still woke to haunting dreams of his father being cuffed and taken into custody while he hid behind his mother's skirts, a frightened child, of his sire wasting away in prison for crimes he didn't commit, while Craymore settled into the Blackstone estate and enjoyed the fruits of his father's labor. He cringed when the image surfaced unwillingly of his mother trying to survive with two young boys in the worst sections of London after being ousted from their home. Her death, painful for him and his brother but a blessing for her, had left them as orphans. They'd survived on the streets as pickpockets and thieves.

They'd refused to beg. Instead they'd used their inherited intellect to become the best in their professions. Martin couldn't help but smile when he thought of York, not even old enough to shave, doing his best to protect his younger brother from the other more street-savvy orphans. York soon learned their tactics, gained their respect and eventually led the pack of miscreants. Their adventures had often brought them to the brink of death, but what adventures they were!

Martin ignored the admiring stares of passersby as he drew closer to the stable he'd rented. Somehow, the thoughts of returning to London had released a barrage of memories that, fortunately, commenced in justice being served.

When the opportunity finally arrived for them to avenge their father's unjust demise, they were well trained and ready to overcome even a man as cruel and devious as Lord Craymore. They'd succeeded. He was dead, the truth revealed. His brother regained his rightful place as the elder. He wanted Martin to be by his side and help him in managing the Blackstone estate. They'd come through hell together and York wanted him to share in all that he'd inherited. Martin couldn't say yes to his brother's offers.

He wanted to make a life for himself. When he left England he'd had no idea what that meant, but he needed to find out. In the months following, he'd met other women here in America very willing to take care of his needs, but none of them aroused the passion he'd felt for Alaina.

Only his thoughts of her helped him to realize that he desired a home and family. He was ready to settle down. He hadn't been prepared to face that responsibility before.

Had she understood his need to leave? He would have had nothing to offer her if he didn't first create a life for himself in which he could feel pride.

And he had only just begun.

He wondered if she'd be willing to leave her world behind. It would be a hard life in Virginia, at least for a time, until he established himself. He wasn't poor but it would take time to create the homestead that he imagined. He wanted her to live in ease and comfort. What if she refused?

As he led the horse into the stables, he thought of Alaina dressed in her simple cream-colored silk gown trimmed with violet ribbons and cut low enough to give a hint of lush breasts. The thought made him burn with desire.

Damn, he thought, as he tried to figure out how much more business needed to be taken care of before gaining passage on a ship back to England. He needed to make another trip to Virginia, meet his overseer and hire trusted men to work on the land while he was gone.

He couldn't leave for at least another couple of months. And while he was traveling back and forth, he'd miss his mail, leaving him wondering if Alaina had responded to his last letter, or even received it. His own need to find himself and create a new life might mean losing the only woman who would make it all worthwhile. And what if she accepted him but refused to leave England? Could he toss away his dreams here in this new land? He pushed away the thought as the horse whinnied, reminding him to stay in the moment.

"EVEN IF WE arrive on schedule, Alaina will have been in America at least two weeks with Harrington. Their ship is already halfway across the Atlantic. I can only imagine what she has already gone through," Richard Craymore muttered to York as he waited to board the next available ship.

"I never thought that he would go to her for what he wanted from me. If I hadn't sent her that letter warning her of my possible arrest, she might not have gone." Richard caught himself from swearing when he remembered Lady Henley's presence, though she stood apart from them, allowing them a private conversation.

"You must stop blaming yourself," York urged. "The man's a manipulator of the worst sort. How could you have known? Keep in mind, your sister may be impulsive and too self-sacrificing for her own good, but she has wits about her and more than an ounce of steel."

"It's her unwavering loyalty to me that's led her into God knows what."

"From our investigations so far, it appears that Harrington has not demonstrated violence toward anyone. He's a boaster and schemer, concerned about his image in the public eye."

"Men change when they are desperate. To think that a woman my sister trusted was involved with him. I should have kept a better eye on Alaina." Richard fisted his hands at his sides.

"Regrets will not help, so put an end to them." York placed a hand on Richard's shoulder. "If Martin isn't off traveling somewhere, he should receive my letter before you reach America. I informed him of what's happened. He won't rest until he finds Alaina."

"You've been a good friend, York. I was too damn young and naïve working with my father. He'd sit at his desk and toss me paperwork to sign or seal. I may have signed papers without reading them closely. I yearned for my father's approval. When I did raise a question, I took his cold demeanor personally, as if I'd erred in asking. My awareness of his true character came too late. I sent that letter to Alaina out of fear that I would be arrested before I could speak with her."

"You did what you thought was best and the documents could very well have been forged." York's voice was nearly blocked out by the sound of the ship's bell. "It's difficult to prove but I have the best lawyers checking into it. Forgery is a criminal offense with a hanging sentence. Experts will be called in to check those signatures. It may well be that Harrington wanted to get out of England because he feared discovery."

"Alaina knows my signature. She must have believed that I'd signed them. I didn't help matters, sending an urgent letter telling her to expect a scandal."

"Do you believe your father actually betrothed her to Harrington?" York asked.

Richard snickered. "He had little respect for women. If it was in his best interest, he might well have promised her to him. We won't know until we see the papers." Richard rubbed his temple. He'd barely slept since he'd heard of his sister's disappearance.

"Perhaps I'll have another talk with Mrs. Dunfly, after you've gone."

"I'm not finished with her. When I return—" Richard clenched his teeth.

"I had an uncomfortable feeling about that woman," Cornelia said, having just returned to their side.

The men turned their attention to Lady Henley.

"Priscilla could seldom look me in the eye." Cornelia was close to tears as she looked up at the two men. "Thankfully, it does appear that Mr. Harrington supplied a chaperone. That is, if the passenger logs are correct."

Richard reached out and took her hand in his to comfort her. "The harbor master assured me that two women boarded with Harrington. Concerning Priscilla, none of us could have concluded that she'd be such a menace. My father kept Alaina so secluded on the estate caring for our mother that she had little time left for friendships. Priscilla must have sensed her loneliness and taken advantage, especially since society chose to scorn my sister for being a Craymore," Richard said. "When I return, she'll answer to me. If I have my way, she will be run out of England."

"According to her, she was manipulated as well," York reminded him.

"She's no victim," Richard growled.

"We need to find out more. There has to be others who would remember him during the time he carried on business with your father, others who were duped by him. I'll continue to find out whatever I can while you're gone."

"I appreciate all you've uncovered, York. I am in your debt."

"You were willing to stand against your father for justice's sake, and Alaina risked her life when she searched for my father's books. I won't forget that. I know that both you and your sister were victims as well. I am indebted to both of you for helping us reveal the truth. No doubt it was as painful for you to face your father's treachery and stand against him as it was for us to face our misfortune."

Richard forced a smile, appreciative of finding

a loyal friend amid inconceivable circumstances.

"I have to add," York said smiling back, "Alaina is like a sister to Marielle. I want her back in England and safe. My wife is distraught over her disappearance, and I am the one who suffers when she is out of sorts."

Richard was reminded of York and Marielle's fiery courtship and Alaina's concern for her happiness. "They were friends long before you and Marielle met. She must be beside herself with worry. I'm sorry that she has to be affected too."

"Marielle is my concern. Focus on Alaina. Perhaps when you arrive in Boston, someone on the docks or a nearby hotel will remember them. Talk to the customs officer. Their arrival should be in his records. I understand that they are doing a better job of keeping track of passenger lists. You can ascertain the name of the ship and if it is not at sea, perhaps talk to the master of the vessel. We know from the records here that Harrington boarded at Liverpool with two women. We can assume that the other woman was the chaperone Alaina mentioned. At least the man had the decency to acquire a female companion."

"What we don't know is if she is a suitable one," Richard scowled.

"I would go with you if I could, find my errant brother as well, but I have too much unfinished estate business."

"And a lovely wife and newborn child," Richard added.

York grinned proudly then grew serious. "Let's hope that my letter is in Martin's hands."

"I have his address, if he's still there. It's a long journey and I know little about America. I have asked enough questions of those who have traveled there and have a rough map of the city. Even with the information I've accumulated, I have no idea what to expect." Richard frowned and looked away.

"You must be more optimistic. Martin's last letter was still from Boston and you have at least one address. I trust that you will find him and if I know my brother, he'll move heaven and earth to find Alaina. Put some trust in your sister too. She is an intelligent young woman who may have allowed her emotions to take over, but I have seen her tenacious will when it's been needed. Remember what she's come through already. She can take care of herself."

"Her reputation...is there any way to salvage it? She must know that leaving with a stranger, regardless if she has a chaperone, will be unforgiveable. She may not want to return to disgrace."

"Richard, Marielle and I have discussed the ramifications of her actions," Cornelia cut in. "We agree that her reputation will be damaged beyond repair, if the ton knows the truth.

"*If?*" Richard drew his brows together. "It would be impossible for her absence to go unnoticed."

"True, but if our plan works, she may escape condemnation. I hadn't planned on saying anything until my niece and I finalize details."

Richard narrowed his eyes at their high-spirited, and often unconventional, companion.

"As you know," Cornelia continued, "Marielle has attended very few functions this past year. Her desire for seclusion will benefit her. Marielle and her husband," she eyed York, obviously expecting his consent, "will pass the word that Alaina has gone to the country to help Marielle with the baby. Will anyone question a lord of the realm? I shall, of course, bemoan her absence to my friends in London and share news of her when I return from my visits with my niece. If Alaina returns by summer's end, the ruse might work. It's worth a try."

Richard listened, astonished at the woman's cunning as well as her unfailing kindness. Not only had she ignored the way society had slighted Alaina but she was scheming to save her from banishment.

"There's little I can say. I appreciate your support. Your plan, however, could place all of you in an uncomfortable position."

"Let us worry about that, young man."

Richard looked toward the boarding platform and saw that most of the passengers were on deck. "I must board. I'll write as soon as I have any news."

"May God speed your journey and grace you with a safe voyage." Cornelia reached up and gave Richard a warm hug.

Richard clasped York's hand before joining the other passengers preparing to embark on their long journey.

As he boarded, he thought about Cornelia's

plan. Would his sister be able to hold her head up
again after all that had happened? What if
Harrington had taken advantage of her innocence?
Knowing his sister's unfair and fragile standing in
society, he questioned if she would ever return.

"MY DEAR, we have reached our destination."

Alaina looked up and down the narrow street
that held a row of identical structures. Though it
was now dusk, the street looked respectable
enough. As she climbed the last few steps to the
Federal-style house, she felt drained, not as weary
from the travel as much as from apprehension of
her days ahead. She watched as Phillip took out a
key.

"Are there no servants about?" she asked,
startled as he unlocked the door.

"My servants do not sleep here most nights,
especially when I am away for long periods. You
will meet Lucia and Maria tomorrow. They are
sisters. Maria does my housekeeping and Lucia
cooks. I will introduce you as a widow and my
fiancée."

"A widow?"

"Less is expected of a widow, as I am sure you
have learned from Priscilla Dunfly."

"You led me to believe that I would have
another chaperone. You have no concern for
propriety?"

"My housekeeper and cook should suffice. At
least one of them will be available to you at all
times." He looked past her to the coachman
unloading their luggage. "Now is not the time to

discuss the protection of your reputation. I have one concern only, your compliance."

Alaina was too tired and defeated to object. As she walked through the door, fear crept up her spine and seemed to circle her throat like a rope. She grasped the stair railing and forced herself to take deep breaths.

To Alaina's relief Phillip was busy with the luggage and hadn't noticed. She refused to appear weak in his presence. Once the luggage was carried in, he paid the coachman and sent him on his way. He lit a lantern by the door and led Alaina through the neatly kept rooms that were furnished sparsely, but with obvious thought to elegance of décor. The main sitting room had a striped wall covering of predominately beiges and browns and the tall windows were draped in maroon velvet. Stiff-looking brocade chairs were angled with a round mahogany table between them. A comfortable couch scrolled in beige and maroon damask was placed against a wall with a large mirror framed in gold leaf above it.

Phillip walked her through a long hallway. "I spend a great deal of time in my library," he said, pointing out a door to his left without opening it. He continued on. "I am very proud of my art collection." He raised a hand to the paintings along the walls. "I hope you will take some time tomorrow to appreciate each piece."

She ignored his suggestion. She had no interest in his art collection, only completing her purpose for being here.

He showed her the dining room, kitchen,

pantry and a small room where his servants slept. "I want you to be comfortable during your stay, Alaina. My servants expected my return this week, so the kitchen should have provisions on hand for this evening if you need a light snack."

They reached the back stairs that led to the second level. He turned about and led her through the hallway again to the main staircase, showing off more of his paintings as they ascended.

"The second floor has three rooms, mine is in there." He pointed to the back room nearest to the stairwell. He stopped at the small center room. "You are welcome to use this one as a sitting area. The front bedchamber will be yours." He led her to it and opened the door.

Alaina held her tongue. The thought of being alone in this strange lodging with him unnerved her. Everything felt so wrong. She must keep Richard's life in the forefront of her mind and pray that she would not lose her own.

Phillip stepped aside to allow her to enter. She noted that the room was neatly appointed but without color. As Phillip went to the stone fireplace to start a fire, Alaina stood apart from him, her arms still gripping her satchel while one foot tapped the wood floor. When Phillip looked her way, she stopped. Phillip returned to feed the flames.

Once he seemed satisfied with the fire, he left to bring up her trunk. His absence gave her an opportunity to look the room over with a critical eye. The ornately carved oak bed was covered with an ecru coverlet. A burgundy afghan lay at the foot of the bed. A dresser and chest were of the same oak design as the bed. A nightstand held a glass-encased candle. The walls in the lamplight looked to be dull beige. A faded green chair sat by the window. She guessed that this room, with its dreary color scheme, was furnished for convenience but seldom used. She laid her satchel down on a chair near the bed and walked over to the fireplace, staring down into the flickering flames.

When Phillip returned, he poked at the fire once more. "There is still a chill in the air, but the fire will help. Springtime in Boston is a lovely time of year. Perhaps tomorrow afternoon I'll show you some of the sights." He smiled that tight smile that she'd disliked from the moment they had met. "Is there anything that you might need tonight?"

Alaina made no reply. She just wanted to be left alone. When he walked to the door, she sighed with relief.

"I must go out for a while to take care of some business," he announced. "I shall return in a few hours. I suspect you will be asleep. I'll notify Maria and Lucia that I have arrived and will expect them in the morning. No doubt my housekeeper will help you unpack and freshen your gowns. Unlike England, you'll not have maids fussing over you. I find servants a burden rather than a blessing."

"Despite designating me as a widow, those you seem so concerned about impressing might question your integrity or my reputation if I live here without a proper chaperone."

"I see you have come to understand my

purposes, Alaina. My associates are aware that I am a bachelor and, therefore, do not expect me to entertain company at my residence. Now that I am engaged, I may need to consider a change in my staff if our business takes longer than expected, but I need not pretend that I believe in all the ridiculous rules that London society feeds on. The privilege of being an American is freedom from the pomp and pickiness of England."

"I find it hard to believe that the new world, despite its battles with Britain and its unique character, has disposed of all of society's traditions."

"Quite true, there are those who refuse to let go of all that poppycock," he snorted. "As I've said, Maria and Lucia will be available for the time being as your chaperones and one of them will accompany us on our excursions. You see, I do have some respect for propriety. I wouldn't want my fiancée's reputation tarnished in the public eye. And by the way, my servants do not speak or understand English. We wouldn't want gossips about, now would we?"

Alaina remained silent, knowing it was useless to argue. She would save her strength for other battles.

"I wish you a good night's rest and I beg you not to allow your curiosity to get the better of you. There are ruffians about the area, just as in London. I wouldn't want you to come to harm." He smiled before closing the bedroom door behind him.

Once he was gone, Alaina unpacked necessary items and heated water over the fire for a sponge bath. She wanted to wash away the dirt and grime from traveling and the darkness she felt in her heart, though she doubted it would help.

As she washed, she wondered what business Phillip would be taking care of at this late hour. Would it have something to do with her? Perhaps he was wasting no time preparing his associates for her arrival.

Numbness had overtaken her once the carriage had stopped at his residence. She hadn't thought to ask about his expectations of the days ahead. Questions assailed her as she undressed, put on her night rail and crawled into bed. Tomorrow she would ask for specifics and a timetable of events.

And then, what?

She squeezed her eyes shut to keep from allowing tears to fall. If she were free to go in a few days, where would she go? She could hardly expect Aunt Cornelia to take her back after leaving so suddenly. She could never explain her reasons for traveling to a country she knew nothing about and with a man she knew nothing of, except that he could destroy her brother.

Only Richard could possibly understand. But would he? Instead of facing imprisonment, he'd be confronted with his sister's shameful actions and her banishment from proper society. Her greatest gift to him might be to stay in America.

Chapter Four

PHILLIP SAT in his library, waiting until there were no sounds of footsteps from Alaina's bedroom directly above him. Since she'd claimed exhaustion, he felt confident that she was asleep. He hadn't planned on going out, but the past few weeks had been grueling. He wanted to check on the girl, Molly, and he needed release with a woman who could meet his needs.

He was tired of acting like the perfect gentleman. Too often lately, he'd wanted to wipe away Alaina's disdainful glares with a slap. He'd done his best to behave admirably so she'd carry through without further coercion, but he was sick to death of catering to her solemn and irritable moods. At least, among others, she'd composed herself.

To meet his deadline, he'd had to neglect his other private enterprise that needed his watchful eye. He wanted to check on it, but even more he needed time with Brigid. He missed her flame-red hair draped over him and the way she contorted her naked body to please him. She would get little rest tonight.

Walking along the dark streets, he reached the alleyway that led to the back entrance of the establishment. Entering the dimly lit hallway, he walked through until he neared the doors that led to the betting parlor. He glanced in but turned away before he could be seen. He never entered the gaming room while patrons were there or talked to the gamblers unless it was under the pretense of being a guest himself. To his workers and to Sophie, his manager and madam of the brothel, he was Mr. Cox. He'd been successful in keeping his true identity from his staff and his paying guests.

He walked past a number of closed doors and down a few steps until he reached a private office. He thrust the door open. Sophie Mae, a plump, heavy-breasted woman with rouged cheeks, jumped from a cushioned chair when she caught sight of him.

"Mr. Cox! Ya surprised me. Didn't expect to see ya tonight."

"I can see that." He glared at the whisky bottle on the table before her, the half-filled glass and the empty nut shells that had landed on her large bosom.

Following the direction of his stare, she dislodged the broken shells caught in the lace around her plunging bodice with a brush of her heavily ringed fingers.

"Why aren't you with the customers? The gaming room is nearly empty."

"Not a big crowd tonight. I gave some of the girls a night off. They ain't had one for a while. Still, not a bad night. Some real gamblin' fools in there. They're throwing money around like it was Christmas. I was just takin' a rest. Everything's been goin' real good. You'll see. Just takin' a break is all."

He grimaced at her sniveling excuses. "I want

to see the books tomorrow night and all the girls back here plying their trade. If the rest of them were here tonight the men would be dropping more cash as well as their britches."

"Yes, Mr. Cox, but things have been going just fine. You'll see."

"How is the girl I sent here today doing?"

"Young Molly Belle? That's what I'm callin' her. She ain't said much except that she wants to go home. She's as green as grass. Was crying when I introduced her to my girls. She don't know what she's gettin' into, does she? She keeps askin' what her position's gonna be. Figured I better not tell her yet that she's gonna be in all kinds of positions." She sucked in a chuckle. "Haven't shown her around yet, just locked her in one of the rooms to rest until I can find time to tell her what we expect. I'll break her in easy."

"She should be thankful that she can pay for some clothes for her grungy brothers and sisters," Phillip shot back. "Her father can't feed all his brats. I took her off his hands."

"She's scrawny but curvy enough to entice our customers. If she'd just keep quiet and stop her sobbin'."

"I'll be here tomorrow night before midnight. Have her in the green room," Phillip ordered. "I'll pay her a little visit and convince her to behave and show some appreciation."

"I understand, Mr. Cox, I do." Sophie gave him a closed-mouth grin.

"Where's Brigid? I want to see her."

"Oh, she's off tonight. Like I said, I didn't

know ya was comin'."

Damn. Brigid knew exactly what he liked and he wasn't in the mood to explain his unusual preferences to an available whore.

"She'd better be here when I arrive tomorrow."

"She'll be waitin', I promise."

"Get back to work." Cursing, he stormed out and left the same way he entered. He walked the remaining blocks back to his house in a worse state than he'd been in before he left.

Better to focus on tomorrow's business.

He'd contact the men involved in the trade agreement, set up an appointment for later in the week and prepare Alaina.

If all goes well, I not only become very rich, but I don't have to accept the paltry portion I'd have received if Craymore had lived. I get it all. That last thought helped to release some of his tension. Fortunately, the brothel and gambling tables brought in a hefty sum and at least, for now, financed his present lifestyle. He wanted more, much more.

Alaina must be convincing. If not, she'll regret her failure.

He'd been considerate and generous in his treatment of her. Innocents weren't to his liking anyway. He had little patience with virgins and he assumed she was one. She was a beauty, a showpiece and perfect for his public image and his bargaining. He'd continue to treat her appropriately as long as she played her part.

If not, she'll owe me. He snickered at the thought of her forced to please some of his customers, especially those with peculiar cravings. In time, she might even be able to satisfy his appetite.

"YOU LOOK elegant, Alaina. You exhibit modesty and dignity in your dress. My associates, no doubt, will be impressed."

Alaina didn't reply. She remained silent as they rode in Harrington's carriage to their first meeting with the businessmen involved in the trade agreement. Her thoughts were consumed with the role she must play. *I represent my father's interests. He deeply apologizes for his inability to travel at this time. He understands your need for a timeline for successful negotiations. Once I return with the signed contract, he will arrange a later meeting.* She continued to revisit all that Phillip expected her to say. She needed to get through this meeting and not suffocate in the fear bottled up inside her.

She'd been in Boston a week and except for strolling with Phillip at his request—she'd viewed it as more of a demand—each afternoon, she never left the apartment. When Harrington met someone on their walks who he wanted to impress, he presented himself as wealthy and polished, though she suspected his means were less than he projected. It was obvious from his behaviors that he craved the distinction of being a part of the inner circle of Boston's elite. Though he was treated with politeness and she with courtesy, she felt a degree of mistrust from some of the more solid citizens. She doubted Phillip noticed. He was too busy posturing. His image was not her concern unless it became an obstacle to the goal.

True to his word, one of the two sisters

accompanied them when they journeyed out, though he introduced her as his fiancée, he never failed to mention in casual conversation that she was widowed. He clearly wanted nothing to mar his image.

This afternoon she was to be introduced to two men from China and their interpreter. Phillip had spent the last two days preparing her for this meeting. He'd explained that the businessmen represented a group of various trade groups in China that sold tea, fabrics and other commodities. Her father and Phillip had begun communications with them and presented incentives for the men to sign a trade contract solely with them. The contract would allow Phillip to mediate between buyers in Boston and eventually other cities interested in their imports. In his arrogance, he bragged about the profits to be made after he negotiated future contracts with the American buyers who would compete with one another, raising the prices of goods as well as the cost of his service.

She didn't care if he was the wealthiest man in America. She wanted to be free of him. Better to face her uncertain future than be in his presence longer than necessary. Her nerves were on edge in all her waking hours and in her sleep she was haunted with terrifying dreams where she was alone in darkness, calling for help and no one answered her pleas. She'd wake sweating and shaking and often clinging to her bed sheets. She'd rise and splash cold water on her face, forcing herself to gain control of her emotions, dress and prepare herself to face the day. Though she wasn't in immediate danger, she felt very much alone and far from the only world she knew.

"Alaina, you appear lost in your thoughts. Keep in mind, my dear, this is simply a meeting of introduction. I have already notified the men of your arrival. They will not expect you to be involved in the more intricate details. Your job is to keep your composure at all costs. You do understand that any action from you that would place doubts in their mind would be disastrous?"

Alaina heard the warning in his voice. As a woman, she knew her place and in this situation, she was glad of her gender. She wanted no part in any of their discussions. All she wanted were the papers incriminating her brother to be destroyed.

"And when will you notify them that my father is dead?"

Harrington's lips curled into a cunning grin. "After the papers are signed, my dear, and they have returned to their homeland. For the time being, let us hope that they accept you."

"And if not?"

Phillip frowned. "Best that we not consider that possibility."

The look on his face silenced her. She'd follow his instructions, demonstrate her loyalty to her father and his concern that they meet their deadline. She'd tell them that he sent her, his only daughter, to represent his interests and with complete faith in his associate, Mr. Harrington, her fiancé, to complete all aspects to the men's satisfaction. She'd assure them that her father looked forward to a long and profitable relationship. Yes, she would say all that was expected and despise every minute of her performance.

When they arrived, Phillip led her into a fashionable dining room at the hotel where the men were staying. As she walked to their table and saw the men, her breath caught. They stood up and bowed, though their eyes appeared cold and their expressions reserved.

Phillip introduced her as Lord Craymore's daughter and his fiancée. The men, though respectful, seemed wary. They asked questions through the interpreter. She responded to each one, explaining that her father's health would not allow him to make the trip, but he was committed so strongly to the venture that he sent her in his stead.

As Harrington had instructed her, she spoke of how pleased her father was about their future marriage. Phillip, with Alaina's smiling assent, told them her father had complete faith in her as a diplomat for his concerns in America, and as a widow, she had gained business prowess through her late husband's ventures. The lies never seemed to stop.

She grew more confident as the meeting progressed and the men appeared more accepting of her presence. When one of the men said something to the interpreter, the mood changed. The interpreter, in broken English, asked Phillip for papers the men appeared to know were forthcoming. Phillip handed them a folder with documents enclosed.

She wasn't privileged to examine the

documents being passed back and forth, but she saw that they made a strong impression on the investors. When the papers were returned to the folder, one of the representatives spoke again to the interpreter who relayed their message.

"My associates are pleased, madam. Your father's letters of guarantee appear in order and his signed approval allows you to represent his interests. You honor your father by traveling a great distance for him. His words demonstrate respect and confidence in your abilities. Time is needed to satisfy all conditions of the contract."

When he finished, one of the other men patted the interpreter's coat sleeve and added a comment. The interpreter smiled for the first time. "They wish you an enjoyable stay in Boston and a long and fruitful marriage." The foreigners grinned. She forced herself to acknowledge their words with a nod, but she said nothing. She was stunned into silence. The men pushed their chairs out, stood, bowed and walked from the room. Phillip waited for her to rise, and led her outside.

It wasn't until they were back in the carriage that she pressed her hands to her pounding heart as she tried to control the rage building within her.

"Alaina, you were magnificent," Phillip said, putting a hand on hers. She brushed it away.

"How could you have produced papers with my father's signature?" Her words came out high-pitched, sounding strange even to her. She was not herself, rather someone she didn't know, someone of whom she was ashamed and worse, someone she feared had been played a fool.

"I found it necessary to have all means of proof of your father's commitment."

"But they had to be forged!"

"And necessary," Harrington said, through gritted teeth.

"And what of the papers that incriminated Richard? Were they also forged?" Alaina's chest heaved. The realization of Harrington's underhanded actions drew her deeper into the horror of what she'd accepted as truth.

"Alaina, only after your brother is arrested, jailed and brought to trial will those documents come under deeper scrutiny. Forgery would be extremely difficult to prove in English courts. I will say no more about it. If all goes well, your brother's papers will be burned in your presence."

Alaina shrunk back in her seat. Thoughts whirled through her mind, Harrington's first appearance, his threats, Priscilla's betrayal, her brother's signature, his letter warning her to prepare for his arrest. She pressed her hand to the door handle. She wanted to escape, to run from this monster, but she had nowhere to go, no one to turn to, and no way to prove the evil she was witnessing. Who would believe her?

Alaina glared at Harrington's arrogant expression. Even if she could find a way to prove forgery had been committed, her brother would suffer. Everything suddenly appeared different, yet nothing had really changed. She had no other choice but to carry through with the pretense until she could figure a way out of this nightmare.

"Straighten up, my dear. We are in full view in

this open carriage. Tomorrow we shall go to a public auction. I'm in the mood to purchase a new carriage."

PHILLIP GLARED up at his stairwell. *If she isn't down here in the next five minutes, I'm going to drag her out of that room.* He'd told Maria, who would accompany Alaina as a chaperone, to wait outside. That had been nearly fifteen minutes ago. He didn't want Maria to be witness to any harsh words between him and his *fiancée*. Though she wouldn't understand the conversation, she'd recognize the hostility.

He was tired but exhilarated. He thought of the few very satisfying hours he'd spent with Brigid until nearly dawn. His body felt raw from her expert ministrations and the tools of her trade. He even agreed to give her the afternoon off since she'd hardly be fit for an energetic tumble with another customer.

He turned his thoughts to Alaina's performance at the meeting the day before. He'd waited until nearly the end of the meeting before producing the forged letter that held her father's signature. The men were too busy examining it to see the shock on her face, only that she'd grown quiet when they'd closed the meeting. They may have assumed that her father's letters reminded her of his illness or absence. Regardless, everything went as planned. He had to give Alaina credit. She'd maintained her composure until they'd left the dining room.

At this point in the negotiations, it mattered

little that she suspected forgery of her brother's papers. Even if he could prove innocence, it would take months, even years to go through the courts. With the Craymore name disgraced and his father's crime still vivid in everyone's minds, Richard could never hold up his head again in proper society. Alaina wasn't ignorant. She knew that to be true.

He pulled out his timepiece. What was taking her so long?

He looked forward to the auction now that he felt more confident of his success. He wanted a more impressive carriage and had heard that some fine horses would be available for bidding. Later they'd stop for tea and go to the Mall. A casual stroll would give him the opportunity to engage in conversations that might benefit him.

Many well-placed Bostonians would be out and about on such a nice day. He could only imagine their lust for exquisite Chinese imports—imports that he would control.

Once the contract was finalized, he would have to decide what to do with Alaina. Now that she knew his well-kept secret, she was a liability.

ALAINA NOTED Phillip's irritation when she descended the stairs. It pleased her to have kept him waiting.

"Erase that dour expression on your face, Alaina. Try to enjoy our outing or at least appear to do so," he grumbled. "The Mall will be crowded, especially after an auction. Future clients advantageous to our venture will be there."

"It is not my venture, it is your deceptive

ploy." She ignored his tight-lipped frown as she tied the ribbons of her bonnet.

"I must say you look exceptionally lovely in that pink gown. You are the picture of springtime," he remarked in a more agreeable tone.

"I would have preferred to wear one of my own dresses."

"Yours are dull, most likely chosen from your mourning closet."

"And Priscilla's are too gay for my taste." She picked at one of the many pink rosettes that trimmed the bodice. "She could have at least packed more subdued colors."

"Enough, Alaina. Come, I want to look over the offerings before the auction begins." He opened the door and offered his arm.

She shrugged and reluctantly accepted it. She nodded to Maria who followed a distance behind them as they walked up the street.

"Good, I see you're wearing sensible shoes," Phillip said. "The Boston streets around the marketplace are poorly kept, filthy in fact, and potholed. You may be spending a good part of your time avoiding stumps in the road as well as refuse."

"Then why did you insist that I wear this frilly gown?"

"To impress the height of Boston's elite."

"And you want them to accept you as one of their own."

Phillip turned his head sharply toward her. "I have had enough of your sarcasm. Until our business is ended, I expect you to appreciate that I have treated you respectfully. I will continue to do so as long as you are compliant to my requests."

"You mean your demands."

"Do not push me too far, Alaina."

She avoided a retort. Her sarcasm was her only defense. She feared him more than ever now that she knew about his forgeries. She'd tried to come up with a plan of escape, but all she'd gained was a headache and a poor night's sleep. She needed to carry through with the ruse.

Even if she sent a letter to Richard, warning him of the forgeries, it would arrive too late to help her and might create more anxiety for him. She could only imagine the worry she'd already caused everyone she'd left behind.

Phillip refused to confirm that the papers he'd presented to her in London were false but she had no doubt. Her heart had told her that her brother couldn't possibly have been involved in smuggling, but his history of working with their father and his letter of warning had made her question everything. She felt ashamed that she'd misjudged him, but what could she have done differently?

She'd foolishly believed Phillip when he said he'd burn the papers that incriminated her brother once she succeeded in the ploy. Now she realized he could make other copies and continue to blackmail her. Her brother would never be free from the threat—and neither would she.

During the night she'd heard Phillip leave the apartment. She hadn't previously cared where he went, only that he was out and she could breathe easier. Now she wondered where his nightly outings took him. Were they clandestine meetings with a forging partner? If she could discover the source of his crime, she may yet prove his deception. That had been her last thought when Phillip had pounded on her door this morning, telling her to hurry up.

When they arrived at the Boston pier, the market bustled with activity. It seemed everyone agreed that it was too lovely a day to remain indoors. Even Maria wore her nicest dress. Shopkeepers were out selling their wares, while men and women bargained with them. Alaina was disgusted to see sheep's and lambs' heads lying on the ground near a butcher shop while well-dressed men and woman simply ignored the sight and chatted as they went on their way.

Many foreigners passed by, talking in their various tongues, while children laughed and tossed balls about. It was at times like these that she could focus on the present and not on her misery. America was truly an amazing land. If the situation had been different, she could imagine coming to appreciate the new world.

Thoughts of Martin intruded her thoughts, bringing tears too close to the surface. She found herself searching the streets for his face in the crowd. She had no idea what she would say or do if she saw him.

It was much too late to hope for his love. She had compromised her decency beyond redemption. What a mess she'd made of her life. She still had nightmares of the night her father died, of the gun slipping from her fingers. The dreams had lessened during the year spent with Aunt Cornelia. She had gained some hope for her future but now she lived in a stranger's home under the guise of being a widow and strolled the streets in a gaudy pink gown. Martin would certainly shun her. Better not to think of him.

When they reached the gates set up where the auction was being held, Harrington drew her to a quieter spot but near enough to watch the goings-on.

"Remain here, Alaina. I must have words with one of the sellers before the carriages go up for auction." He waved a hand toward a bench that had one remaining seat available. "Do not move from this place. You know what is at stake if I can't find you when I return."

Alaina's mouth thinned but she nodded her acquiescence. When Harrington strode off, she signaled for Maria to take the empty seat. The woman was older and Alaina preferred to stand and observe the crowd. As the minutes went by the crowd grew. She glanced toward her chaperone, though she had to rise up on her tiptoes to have the bench in view. She was surprised to see Maria in an animated conversation with another woman. Their hand gestures suggested their own excitement over the venue. How she wished that she could find a friend in this mob of foreigners.

That was her last thought before clutching her throat. *Martin.* He was there in the crowd, standing taller than those about him. Her eyes grew wide as she watched him saunter casually toward where she stood. He hadn't seen her. She watched his agile gait, his expression, one of expectation, even determination as he strode closer. She opened her mouth, then clamped it shut again. She clenched her fingers into the folds of her skirt—she didn't know what to do. Should she run to him, plead for his help, or hide? Instead of doing either, she stood paralyzed. She couldn't believe that it was truly him. He drew closer and his eyes darted in her direction. He stopped when he saw her, nearly causing a man behind him to stumble back into the crowd.

She saw the disbelief in his features as he pushed his way through the throng, his eyes never leaving hers. She didn't move, every ounce of her being wanting to run to him, while a warning within her kept urging her to flee.

"Alaina? By God, it's really you." He rushed to her side, breathless, grasping her upper arms. "What are you doing here?" He scanned her surroundings. "Who are you with? I can't believe you're here."

She stared up at him, the sensation of his strong hands on her arms, rapturous. She didn't want the warmth that encompassed her to end. She dared to lift her fingers and grasp his forearms, feeling the heat of his body beneath his shirtsleeves. Her lips trembled. She had to get hold of herself, say something.

"Martin," she finally breathed. "I-I, I never expected to see you. Richard…" she swallowed as the story she must tell him formed in her mind. "I have come with my brother. He is here to handle some business affairs. He is in there." She pointed past the gates, in the direction where Phillip had disappeared. "He wanted to look at the items at auction. He preferred I wait here." She was amazed that she could utter even a sound or put a sentence together. She'd believed she could fall no further, yet she'd become worse than disgraced, she'd become a shameful liar. Would he believe her? She continued, the words invented as she uttered them. "My maid came along and is over there, on the bench." She waved a hand, thankful the bench was now fully hidden by the crowd moving forward.

"Alaina, I have thought of you often. And to see you here, I'm speechless. Are you...how was your voyage? How long have you been in Boston?"

She realized that he was as tongue-tied as she and just as shocked at their meeting. Somehow, she needed for him to leave her. Her prayer had been answered only for her to realize how futile it was. As soon as she'd spoken her brother's name, only seconds before, she had regained her senses and her purpose. She could not involve Martin, not now. Phillip would return at any minute. She feared his reaction if she saw them talking. She had to complete her mission alone and deny her dreams.

"We have been here only a few days and will return shortly." Good, her voice sounded less strange to her.

"You must not have gotten my last letter then, if you were aboard ship."

"No, only one, telling me that you arrived safely and were planning to look for land." *Please, you must go*. She needed to urge him to leave, though her heart wanted him to stay.

"Yes, I purchased land in Virginia. You would be amazed, Alaina, at the untouched beauty of the place. I've hired an overseer to begin the cultivation of the land and the buildings."

Alaina couldn't miss the excitement that shown on his face and in his eyes. He was meant to be here, she thought, unlike her, who yearned to escape and return home.

"I am happy for you," she finally said, offering him her first smile. "You must want to see Richard and get on with your business."

"I can hardly believe that you're actually here. I'll find Richard so we can go somewhere quiet to talk. I have so much more to tell you." He lifted a hand and brushed her cheek, before appearing to realize that they were in public.

"Go, find him now, Martin. I'll remain here." She let her gaze linger on his face, on his lips that were slightly parted, on his eyes that were searching hers. *Had he truly missed her too?*

"You'll stay here then. I'll find him and we'll go somewhere quiet. I have so much to tell you." He delayed in letting go of her arm. Finally, he released her and turned away, glancing back as if to be certain she remained.

She watched until he disappeared into the crowd. *Phillip, where are you? We need to get out of here, now.* She found her way back to the bench and discovered Maria still chatting in her own language with the woman who now sat beside her. She grinned happily at Alaina before her gaze went to someone behind her.

Alaina turned to see Harrington approaching. Her heart dropped in her chest while at the same time relief flooded her. He'd arrived before Martin returned.

"We can move on, Alaina. I've secured a nice deal and will not need to wait for the auction to begin." He took her arm and led her away from the auction gate. Maria followed obediently close behind.

MARTIN'S BODY was charged with exhilaration and anticipation. He hurried from booth to booth, from one seller to another but saw no sign of Richard. He continued to search, his thoughts remaining on Alaina. She was actually here, in Boston. He had so much to say to her. He wanted to apologize for leaving England in haste and without even a personal visit to discuss his plans or offer an appropriate farewell.

As he looked about, something nagged at him. She appeared different. Though he was certain that she was pleased to see him, she seemed tense, on edge, even anxious for him to leave. He recalled how her eyes at times seemed to absorb his and as quickly her gaze turned toward the gate, suddenly appearing anxious. Had her brother left her there waiting too long? Being in a strange place, she may have become worried at his disappearance.

She'd said that they'd only recently arrived. She must be exhausted from the trip. He knew well enough that the voyage could be hazardous and many passengers became seasick or worse along the way. He had wanted to ask her about the trip, but he thought that could come later, once they could sit together and really have a long conversation. She most likely hadn't seen much of Boston yet or rested enough to truly enjoy the new world. He didn't want to believe that too much had changed between them. Their attraction to each other had been real enough, but his need to escape England had overtaken his desires. Only after he'd left her behind, even spent nights with other women, did he realize how much she'd meant to him.

Frustration grew as he continued his search for her brother. Could he have already returned to Alaina? They might be there waiting for him. He took one last look around and turned back toward the entrance gate. It took him a good fifteen minutes to return to where he'd found her. Others stood there, and she was gone.

He searched the crowd in every direction. *Why did they leave?* Had he imagined their conversation? No, she was as real as the touch of her hands on his arms that stayed with him even now. He remained near the spot where she'd stood as minutes past, not knowing what to make of it.

Why hadn't he asked where they were staying? He would check every hotel in the vicinity until he found them. But why would they leave? Wouldn't she have told Richard to wait? He scratched his head. Then he remembered that he'd sent his address in his letters to both Richard and Alaina. Richard must have had an appointment of some kind. He couldn't leave Alaina behind. That had to be it. He would certainly contact him before they left Boston.

Feeling some relief, while remaining anxious, he reentered the gates, having caught the sight of a stallion earlier that would go to bid. He recognized the sleek black horse with the white streak on its forehead before seeing the seller. The horse was a beauty and would sire some exceptional colts. Within minutes he bargained for a good price and paid the owner who helped him lead the horse out of the auction area.

The crowd that stood about stared at the magnificent creature he'd purchased. He wasn't surprised. Here was a horse descended from superb stock that would be a prize to own, though few who hung about watching could afford him.

"Have you a stable to keep him that caters to thoroughbreds, Blackstone?" the owner, Mr. Randolph, asked as he walked with him, holding one side of the horse's bridle.

"Temporary accommodations have been made. I've recently purchased property in Virginia and have hired a trainer. Unless plans change, I'll be taking him there as early as next week," Martin said as he stroked the horse's mane.

"You know how to work a good bargain, young man, and you have the air of an aristocrat. I'd like to do more business with you."

The horse skittered back, straining against the holds on his bridle, when a disturbance began nearby. "What the devil? I'll be right with you, Randolph." Martin gave little thought to those around him when he grabbed the collar of the man who was brazenly grappling at a young woman who could hardly defend herself. He tossed him to the ground. The short, round-bellied man, looked Martin over, no doubt recognizing his superior size, and backed up. Scrambling to his feet, he ran.

An older woman with bright-red hair, too much makeup and a very revealing dress, confronted Martin. "Best you mind your own business, mister." She looked him up and down, her red lips breaking into a smile. "Unless, you desire some pleasurable entertainment? You are a looker." She wiggled a hip closer to his.

Martin took the woman's measure. She was obviously a prostitute out looking for clients.

"Not interested, ma'am." He stepped away.

"Then leave us be," the redhead said, appearing insulted. She grabbed the younger woman's arm. "Molly, come on now. It's time we got back."

The younger woman, who looked fragile and more like a child than a woman, appeared new to the profession, though her dress fit the line of work. Martin thought he saw fear in her eyes as the redhead pulled her away. *She'll be none too happy with the treatment she'd eventually come to accept*, he thought ruefully. He wondered if she had gone into the trade willingly.

"May I interest you in a fine mare or a handsome Morgan that will take your breath away?" Randolph asked, regaining Martin's attention when he returned. "They're a hefty price but they're worth every penny."

Martin laughed, for he knew if he found the horses to his liking, the wrangling would begin.

"Once this horse is settled, I need to return to my rooming house. I hoped to be meeting with some friends, new arrivals from England."

Randolph nodded with understanding. "Always nice to see old friends arrive. Here is my card. If you find yourself free later, come by my place and we'll go for a drink and discuss further business. I can see you're a man of principle, Mr. Blackstone." His eyes went to the two women who were disappearing into the crowd. "I'll tell you what I have to offer. There's an establishment not too far from here that caters to men of good taste as well as housing some comely whores, friendlier than those two. If that's not to your liking, we can enjoy a good card game or two."

Martin had no reason to tell him that he'd just seen the woman he hoped to marry and had no interest in any other female company.

"What do you say?" Randolph interrupted his musing. "A game of cards? I wouldn't mind winning the money I lost in agreeing to your price."

"Or, if I play my cards right," Martin chided, "I may end up with an even better deal. I'll contact you if my plans change." They shook hands and Martin walked away, anxious and hopeful that he would soon see Alaina again.

"WE MUST leave," Phillip said abruptly, pulling at Alaina's arm. He maneuvered her through the crowded marketplace while Maria struggled to keep up.

"Why the sudden rush?" Alaina asked, trying

to free herself from his tight grasp.

"I forgot some business. I must attend to it immediately," he muttered, barely loud enough for Alaina to hear.

The last thing he needed was Richard Craymore snooping around Boston looking for them and he was certain that he'd recognized him in the crowd. Alaina must have said something before she left or wrote to him. Or was it Priscilla? The deal could be completed in a week and he'd have no more need of Alaina. Her brother's interference could ruin everything.

He cursed. Maybe it wasn't him. Had he become paranoid now that he was so close to gaining all that he'd dreamed of? They'd been in Boston over two weeks. It was possible for Richard to have boarded a ship while they were at sea and arrive by now.

He couldn't be certain if it had been him or not. He'd reacted too quickly, leaving without a second look.

Meanwhile, he needed to figure out what to do if Richard appeared at his door. *Craymore has his father's blood. Perhaps if I offered him a partnership he'd overlook my method of securing his cooperation. How important was a sister compared to the benefits he'd accrue? I'd lose sizeable profits but it might be necessary.* How could the man refuse?

For now they needed to get out of sight. He wasn't going to take any chances. Rather than walk the distance to his house, he signaled for a coach.

"Phillip, I'd like an explanation," Alaina demanded. "You rushed us away as if you'd seen a ghost."

"I told you I have *business*." He didn't wait for the coachman to reach the door. He pulled it open and rushed the women inside before climbing in and slamming the door behind them.

When they arrived back to the apartment, Maria scurried off to the kitchen, but Alaina stood her ground. "Phillip, what was that all about? I think I deserve an explanation."

"I don't need to give you justifications for any of my actions," Phillip snarled. "Get out of my sight." He pushed her aside and went straight to his library, slamming the door behind him.

Craymore's death had created enough complications. He was sick to death of the entire family. Had it truly been Alaina's brother? Perhaps he should have stayed to verify the man's identity, now there was no way for him to know if it was really him.

He was too close to achieving his goal. The letter he had forged with the elder Craymore's signature had been a stroke of genius. Though the men had no desire to deal with a woman, Alaina's presence had solidified his bargaining position. The men were even discussing a larger investment. Alaina's brother could ruin everything or, worse, demand too large a portion of the profits.

Phillip pushed his chair out from beneath his desk and sat down heavily, rubbing his forehead. The anxiety over Richard's reaction to his blackmail was giving him a blasted headache.

"I can't let anything or anyone stand in my way. I've worked too hard for this." He thought of the rumors that had begun floating about before he'd left for England. With Craymore's daughter by his side, previous suspicions that he'd been connected to an illicit operation, the brothel most likely, seemed to have diminished. He'd laughed at the accusations when confronted with them, but he wasn't sure that the rumor had completely run its course.

He straightened and shuffled some papers around before slamming his fist down on his desk.

MARTIN HELD the harness of his new stallion, leading him toward the stable. He wanted to secure him and return to his apartment. Though he doubted that Richard and Alaina would be there waiting so soon, he wanted to notify his landlord that the two may be arriving at any time. "Blackstone! Here!"

Martin jerked his head toward the direction of the voice. *By God, it's Richard!* He watched him mill his way through the crowd toward him.

"Thank God, I've found you!" Richard shouted.

"And you!" Martin slapped him on his back, happy to see him before looking behind him."

"Where's Alaina?"

Richard caught his breath. "It's a long story. I can't believe I've found you. God must be with me."

Martin saw the strain on Richard's face and noted his haphazard appearance. "Come. I need to get this creature safely stabled. Has Alaina returned to your hotel?"

Richard gave him an odd look. "Alaina isn't with me, Martin. That's why I'm here. To find her. She is in danger."

Martin's brow creased in confusion. "What are you talking about? I just saw her. She told me you were in the auction and would be joining her. I thought—"

"You saw her? *Where?*" Richard grabbed Martin's shirt, the muscles in his neck strained as he face reddened.

"At that auction gate. Richard, what the hell is going on?"

"She left England with a man, a stranger."

"What the devil are you talking about?" Martin shouted then subdued his rage as the horse whinnied and sidestepped away from him. "I just saw her, damn it. She said she was waiting for you."

They had reached the stable and the owner stood in front, waving for him to lead the horse into his stall. Martin was forced to deal with stabling the stallion before rejoining Richard.

"I need to go back to the auction. Maybe I'll see her," Richard said, his voice quivering.

"She's no longer where I left her. She promised she'd wait." Martin shook his head, bewildered and now fearful for Alaina. "We'll go back together, but tell me everything, now!"

As they walked, Richard told him the whole story.

"I never received York's letter," Martin cursed. "I've been away from Boston. How could your sister leave England without telling anyone, and with a stranger?"

"She believes she's protecting me, saving me from prison. None of it makes sense. Martin, I know you are fond of my sister, but there are things you don't know about her. She has a sacrificial nature and has always had deep devotion and loyalty to our mother and to me. With the turmoil in our household, Alaina's needs remained in the background. She should have been able to enjoy a coming-out, parties and balls. Instead she nursed my mother until her death, all while trying to protect her from my father's inconsistent behaviors."

"But she is sacrificing her own life, never mind her reputation." Martin couldn't hold back the accusation in his voice. He had to remind himself that he was talking to her brother, who was obviously distraught.

"Alaina suffered more than I did from my father's tempers. He was physically abusive to my mother, never harming her in a way that society would notice, but he thought nothing of pushing her to the floor, even stepping on her as she tried to pull herself up. When Alaina was a small child, she would grab him by the legs to pull him away, only to get swatted by him. His rages were usually short lived. He'd stomp out of the room and return as if nothing had occurred and expect everyone to behave as if all was fine. When our mother became bedridden, Alaina stayed by her bedside day and night. She had no life of her own, few friends, none that were allowed to visit. Only Marielle, your brother's wife, knew anything of Alaina's impossible situation."

As Richard talked, Martin saw the worry and exhaustion on his face. They both continued to scan the area as Richard went on with barely a pause. Martin's stomach churned in disgust as he absorbed the details of Alaina's early life. Even he had abused her by satisfying his need to hold her in his arms, to kiss her, only to leave her behind without a word.

Richard seemed to realize that Alaina must have left the area just as Martin himself arrived at the same conclusion. They found a bench that offered some privacy. Both slumped into it. Martin recognized the look of desperation on Richard's face. He felt it inside his gut and had no idea what to do with it. He needed to figure out how to find Alaina. He turned his attention back to Richard, who continued on as if he were speaking to himself.

"As my father's son, I drew more favor than my sister and I admit, I desired it for too long, even when I matured enough to realize the evilness of his actions."

"Richard, it's understandable. A son looks to his father. Your behavior was normal."

"Alaina saw me as her protector yet I failed her. Eventually I learned how to pull my father's attention away when he turned his anger on Alaina. I know that my sister worshiped me in those moments, but the truth is it was her courage that helped me to stand up to him. As she grew older, she could remain calm, yet portray such strength that even our father realized that she could stare him down without saying a word."

Martin shook his head, stunned by Richard's admissions. Alaina had been forced to learn ways of survival rather than live with love and security, not so unlike him and his brother. She may have had a roof over her head, but she faced as much chaos and terror.

"After the court proceedings were over," Richard continued, "I saw the change in Alaina. While I was busy this past year settling my father's final affairs and rebuilding my business reputation, she drew into herself. She seemed to have created a place inside where she found peace. It's hard to explain." Richard's remorseful expression turned to puzzlement. "She had no desire to go anywhere. I could understand that. Society can be so cruel, especially to a woman whose family name carries such abhorrent scandal."

"Did she remain with Lady Henley?"

"Yes. Thank God for that blessed woman. Under her care I believe that my sister had begun to emerge from the shell she'd wrapped around her. If I hadn't grown so busy trying to redeem my own reputation, she might have confided in me more. I might have even been there when Harrington appeared. She tossed her reputation and her life aside to protect me."

"Don't blame yourself, Richard. Both of you were brought up in a home without secure grounding. Protecting each other came before propriety. Actually, it was no different with York and me. Survival came first. There was no justice in our world. Alaina's first instinct would be to protect you rather than cater to society or fear their scorn."

Richard breathed in a deep sigh. "I don't know where to begin to search for her. I arrived late yesterday and found a hotel room. Today I've just walked around, looking at faces as if in a fog. I have no direction or plan to execute. I went to the docks to find the shipping company that Alaina sailed on but I was told to come back on Monday to ask my questions. It appears the big auction has gathered people not only from Boston but surrounding areas. I mentioned Harrington's name to a few people but many don't live in Boston and none knew of him."

Martin clasped his hand behind his head and looked up to the sky, trying to figure out a plan of action and not reaction. He wanted to ride across Boston, check every house and every storefront until he found her, but he'd learned long ago not to react to situations but rather to consider all angles.

"You look tired, Richard. Why don't you go back to your hotel, get some rest. Tell me where you're staying. I'll see what I can find out and get back to you."

"I'm at the City Hotel, but no, I won't rest until I have something to go on."

"Being a Saturday, and as late as it is, it will be difficult to find the right people to talk to. Sunday may be no better. Church takes precedence over all other affairs. We might be able to get information on Harrington at City Hall Monday morning."

"There must be something we can do before then."

Martin clawed through his hair, now damp from sweat. He kicked at a stone with his heel before suggesting his idea, which held little promise, but it was better than doing nothing.

"The man who sold me that stallion wanted to meet tonight at a gaming hall. He might know of Harrington since it appears that the scoundrel may have been the one who told Alaina to wait at the gate. It's a long shot, but Randolph may have even spoken with him if he was looking to buy a horse. If not, others out for a game of cards or female company might know the name. It's a better opportunity to ask questions than on the streets. If you won't take my advice and rest, then why not accompany me?" Martin pulled out the man's card for his address. "We might get lucky. A gambling establishment might be just the place to ask some leading questions or get some names that might be helpful. Better not to reveal the reasons. We might end up talking to someone loyal to Harrington. Anything's possible. We need to be careful."

Martin rose from the bench. "We'll find her, Richard, I promise you that, but as in any city, locals protect their own and corruption exists. We're the strangers."

As they walked through the streets, Martin's thoughts tortured him. His Alaina, the woman who haunted his dreams, who he'd left behind to seek adventure, was in trouble. When he'd held her in his arms and kissed her on the terrace of the Blackstone estate, she'd responded in her innocence with passion. Though no words had been spoken, he had hoped she would understand his need to leave and would trust that he would return. What a fool he'd been. She had lived with too much trauma, the circumstances of her father's death still with her and the life she'd known previous. He'd only added to her unhappiness.

The truth was that he had wanted her as his own even then, but his reckless need for adventure drove him. Or had it been the need to leave behind the Blackstone-Craymore scandal and all it entailed? Regardless, he had never forgotten her and would have returned to her eventually. He had been overconfident that she would be waiting for him, even willing to follow his dreams. He felt assured that her home with Cornelia Henley gave her a secure place to heal. Instead, his leaving had allowed Harrington to take advantage of her innocence.

She couldn't know what he'd learned about himself, that what he'd gained in his travels meant nothing without her. He'd longed to hold her again and wanted to see if the sparkle he'd seen in her eyes for him would still be there. He'd hoped that now that her year of mourning was over, she'd consider a new life with him in America.

He'd stayed away from England too long — long enough for Alaina to get herself into trouble. His guilt at not being close by when she needed him ate at his insides. And now her willingness to sacrifice her reputation, even her life, for her brother, only made him want her more.

He wanted to marry her and be her protector.

Would she agree to stay in America with him? He wanted to build his ranch, raise children and live far away from the revulsion of the London streets where he and his brother had been forced to live as orphans and thieves. He needed her by his side, but how could she know that when he'd left so suddenly. He had feared if he'd faced her before he left, that he'd change his mind, not be able to leave.

His insides twisted in rage. He would find Phillip Harrington. His hands fisted as he thought of what he would do to him.

Chapter Five

ALAINA SAT on her bed, wearing her darkest gown and her black, hooded cape. She'd been waiting close to an hour for Phillip to leave the apartment as he did most nights. If he didn't leave soon, she feared her growing anxiety would shatter her courage. She needed to know if his nightly visits were to meet a counterfeiter, someone who might hold the evidence that would prove her brother innocent if Phillip attempted more blackmail.

She sensed his growing impatience over closing the trade deal and with his volatile behavior today, she feared even more for her safety. She could no longer allow Phillip to control her every move. Maria had gone home and Lucia, the cook, would be asleep by now in her room behind the kitchen. The house was quiet and it had to be close to midnight.

She stiffened when she heard footsteps below. She waited for the sound of the front door to be unlatched before rising from the bed. Collecting her nerve, she tiptoed out of the room to the stairs and listened before taking each step slowly. The lower hall was empty. She opened the door and peered out into the dimly lit street. Phillip was already near the end of the block.

Waiting until he turned the corner, she slipped out, shut the door quietly, and followed him, trying to stay in the shadows. She was thankful that no one was about. At one point, when a carriage went by, he turned around. She scrambled behind a nearby bush and waited for the carriage to pass. She emerged from her hiding place and continued to follow. He turned and disappeared into an alleyway. She followed more slowly and slipped into the same passageway unnoticed.

Stepping cautiously in the darkness, she nearly stumbled on discarded bottles. Afraid the clatter of the glass might have drawn attention, she slipped behind a barrel. She sighed with relief. Silence surrounded her and Phillip was nowhere to be seen. She crept forward, keeping close to the side brick wall until she spied a door. There was no other way out of the alley. He'd have had to enter it.

She pushed aside her fear and reached for the handle. It was unlocked. She opened the door and slipped through, pressing her back against the wall in the dark hallway. She stepped sideways cautiously until she found a hidden alcove. From her hiding place she saw a large well-lit room, its two entrance doors opened wide. Men's rowdy voices filled the air. She could see them sitting around tables, playing cards, while women dressed in provocative gowns sat on their laps or hung about them.

A large-breasted woman dressed in layers of bright purple appeared in the adjoining hallway and stood to the side of the gaming room doors. Thankful for the darkness, Alaina pressed her slim figure flat against the wall. The men's voices made it difficult for her to hear the woman, but she could see well enough. Her plunging neckline and brassy hair left little doubt of her occupation.

Alaina closed her eyes briefly, trying to swallow her disappointment. There was no sign of a forgery operation here. It was a gambling hall and most likely a brothel. *So this is where he satisfies his lust.* At least he had kept their bargain and left her alone. She felt some appreciation for the women.

"Mr. Cox, there ya are. I think you might like to see this," the woman in purple said to a man joining her. Alaina's eyes widened. She stifled a gasp. It was Phillip, but why was she calling him Mr. Cox? Alaina listened, her palms pressed against the wall.

"There's a man who's taken a likin' to Molly Belle and she ain't been rude or pretendin' she was sick."

Phillip, staying out of sight of those in the room, peered in.

"See, he looks well polished, don't he?" The woman smiled.

Phillip smirked as he watched from his darkened vantage point and spotted their quarry. "Haven't seen him before, Sophie, but he looks flush enough in the pockets. Let him pay a hefty price for her. Might make up for some of the aggravation she's caused," Phillip grumbled.

Alaina absorbed every sickening word as the realization hit her. Phillip, or Mr. Cox as he was called, was obviously in charge. She wanted to turn and run but feared being seen. She prayed they'd move away from view so that she could slip out unnoticed.

"He's with two other men, one's a regular," the woman said. "I'll go urge our Molly to coax him out. He's been a big winner tonight. Wouldn't hurt to get him away from the tables for a time."

"We might as well get some of his winnings. Tell Molly to get busy or she won't eat for a week," Phillip muttered.

"Ain't goin' to save any money. That girl barely eats as it is," Sophie said with a throaty laugh.

Phillip remained in the darkness of the hallway, watching intently as the woman he called Sophie entered and swayed over toward a corner table, stopping briefly at other tables and laughing jovially as one man swatted her on her generous behind.

Alaina's mind was racing. *Molly? Could it be the same girl I traveled with? Is this the position he promised her?* She felt sick at the thought. She needed to get out of here. It was not what she'd expected at all. Her situation grew more dangerous by the moment. Phillip was far worse than a money-hungry businessman.

She stayed frozen in place, watching and listening. Phillip remained in the hallway, viewing the room as the woman in purple circled around the corner table where four men sat. She stood behind one of the men and carried on a conversation with him.

Alaina inched closer, remaining out of sight. The man who the woman was talking to caught her attention. Though his face was turned away, he reminded her of Martin. His hair was dark and curled up at the nape of his neck, just as she remembered. She couldn't help but stare, mesmerized. How she'd searched for his face in every crowd. Was it wishful thinking to hope she'd found him again, her fears and desires colliding with reality?

Sophie took a step back and reached for the arm of a girl who had stood to the side, partially our of Alaina's view. The man stood. He was tall and lean like Martin. She was captivated by the remote possibility that she could be seeing him again so soon.

She darted a look toward Phillip, who remained watching the scene. What if he turned around and decided to leave the establishment, or what if someone entered the back door? She should get out of here but she was trapped in her curiosity and her longing for the man she loved and needed so desperately. She kept staring, noting the familiar broad shoulders so like Martin's. The man turned, his eyes directed at the girl, but his face was now in full view. She crushed her hand to her lips.

Martin.

She couldn't doubt herself any longer, his eyes, the curve of his lips, his strong chin. She wanted to call out, but she couldn't. She'd once again have to stay silent about her predicament, just as she had done earlier in the day.

She remained unmoving—she couldn't reveal herself. Seeing Phillip's back to her as he continued to leer into the room was enough of a warning. There was nothing she could do but take in the sight of Martin as tears streamed down her face.

The young girl drew closer to Martin and snuggled against him, her head turning and resting on his chest.

Oh my God, it is Molly.

She heard the larger woman laugh before she swayed her hips and walked away and back out the door to where Phillip waited. Alaina couldn't tear her eyes away from the sight of Martin and the girl. Sophie's loud voice pulled her from her fixed gaze.

"Molly Belle appears to be lightin' up with this one, Mr. Cox. She has good taste too. He's one handsome devil."

"Make certain she doesn't scare him away. If she does, I'll see to it that she pays for the aggravation she's caused. She'll be on her back for a week until she begs me to let her do her job."

"Yes sir. Don't ya worry, I'll see to it," Sophie said, moving away.

Alaina wiped away her tears. Nothing could have prepared her for this night. She had to leave now. She didn't want to think of what would happen to her if she was discovered, but how could she walk away from Martin again?

Thankfully, Phillip turned from the door and walked down the opposite hall. As soon as he was out of sight she turned and fled out the door and ran through the alley. Her heart pounded in her chest as she tried to wipe away the tears that refused to stop. She ran through the streets. She'd never felt so alone and desperate.

She reached the tenement house and stopped at the door to catch her breath, forcing herself to open it quietly. She slipped in and climbed the stairs. When she reached her bedroom, she flung open the door, closed it and pressed her back against it, her breath heaving. She threw herself on her bed, curled into a tight ball and allowed the tears of rage and sorrow to fall freely.

When her tears were spent, she dried her eyes, stretched out and stared at the ceiling for a long time until her body shook from cold and damp. Realizing the fire had died out hours before, she rose and put logs and kindling in the fireplace and stoked the coals until they turned red. She waited for the wood to catch, rubbing her cold arms.

Finding a shawl, she wrapped it around herself and sat in a chair near the fireplace and rocked slowly, staring into the flames. She conjured up the image of Martin as he stood in the gambling hall while Molly, dressed like a harlot, smiled up at him.

What could I have said? Martin, I am living in Boston with the man who runs this sordid establishment? She let out a bitter laugh. And what about Molly? Had she known that Phillip was bringing her to America to work as a prostitute? Alaina doubted it.

The daydreams that had stayed with her since her arrival in Boston, dreams of seeing Martin on a street corner, or in a park...foolish dreams had been snatched away from her in a day.

Martin was not her savior.

She whisked away another tear with the palm of her hand. Harrington, Cox...who was this man who had blackmailed her into coming to America?

What have I gotten myself into and where do I go from here?

She closed her eyes and rocked steadily back and forth, her mind replaying the confusion, a cluttered collage of her impulsiveness, her fears and her regrets.

She considered the days ahead. She had chosen her fate. Tonight she'd mourn her loss but tomorrow she would face the day with new eyes. She could no longer wait and pray for Phillip's business deal to be completed or believe in his promises of her return to England.

She would write letters to her brother, Cornelia, York and Marielle, explain her actions and her whereabouts. She'd find a way to get the letters on a ship to England as soon as possible. She'd run away. She'd see if she could sell her jewelry for passage home. She stopped, her bravado weakening. Phillip still had the papers, the evidence against Richard. If she could only find them and destroy them.

Fear clutched at her throat while the room closed in on her and the unwanted tears continued to flow unbidden and unstoppable.

RICHARD ROSE from the gaming table to stretch his legs. The strain of the long voyage and his fears for his sister were taking their toll. Over the past year, he'd managed to gain control of his own life and prove his worth apart from his father's disgraced legacy. Now none of what he'd accomplished had any value. He'd neglected Alaina, entrusted her to the care of Lady Henley and felt assured that she was finally safe from their father's cruelty. If he'd only heard Harrington out when he'd appeared at his door instead of refusing to give his time.

Richard had refused to listen. He'd been late in leaving for Chelsea and he hadn't been in the mood to hear one more story from a disgruntled previous associate of his father. He'd spent enough time on his deceitful affairs. He hadn't even planned to read the papers that Harrington had handed to his butler. He could never have imagined that the swindler would seek out his sister and use her to reap his profits.

He had reluctantly agreed to join Martin and Randolph at the gambling hall. Walking the streets and asking strangers about Harrington had proved ineffectual and in Martin's view, possibly dangerous, especially if he approached someone loyal to Harrington.

The last few hours were a waste. He had carried on mundane conversations with gamblers, leaving it to Martin to bring up Harrington's name. Martin had warned him that any frantic note in his voice might alarm someone in collusion with their prey. They'd learned nothing and he needed fresh air.

As he reached the doors of the smoky room, he thought his eyes were deceiving him. The brightly dressed woman he'd observed strutting about the gambling hall was whispering to someone who looked too much like the man who stood in the foyer of his London townhouse, Phillip Harrington. He retreated back into a hidden corner near the door so he could watch the two of them converse.

"It is him," Richard muttered. Fortunately, those around him were too wrapped up in their games to hear him. He wanted to leap at the monster and demand to know what he had done with his sister, but he remembered Martin's warnings. He scanned the room. Too many people were around, including strongmen hired to keep order. Restraining himself, he watched as the woman turned Harrington's attention to someone in the room.

He realized that the object of their interest was Martin. They were eyeing him and the young trollop who stood near him. Harrington appeared to be giving the woman, probably the madam of the brothel, orders. She left him, entered the room, and walked casually over to Martin. He watched her take the young girl's arm and introduce her to his friend. After a brief conversation, she left them alone.

To his disbelief, Martin drew an arm around the girl and led her away from the tables and out the gaming room doors. He suppressed his rage and his desire to go after him but Harrington hadn't moved. How could Martin think about tumbling a prostitute when Alaina's life was at stake?

He noticed that Harrington stayed hidden in the darkness. He wasn't surprised. Most men who desired recognition in society choose not to be associated with a gaming hall and brothel.

The madam rejoined Harrington and spoke a few words to him before reentering the room. Harrington turned and walked away.

Looking about the room to be sure no one's eyes were on him, Richard walked out. He spied Harrington turning down an adjoining hall. Martin and the girl were at opposite end of the main hallway, her hands clinging to his shoulders. With anger rising in his chest, he thought to go after Harrington alone and leave Martin to his whore. Instead, he hurried over to them.

"I saw him," he blurted out, ignoring the girl's surprise.

"Harrington?" Martin's stepped out of the girl's hearing.

"He was obscured behind the door, watching the gamblers. I'm going after the bastard."

"*Wait*," Martin urged in a rough whisper. He stepped back to Molly's side and whispered something to her before rejoining him.

"You can't start a ruckus, Richard. If those guards hear a scuffle, they'll come running. Show me where he went and force yourself to remain calm."

Richard gritted his teeth and led him through to the hall where Harrington had disappeared.

"Hey, where are you going?" a deep voice called out. "That's a private exit."

Richard ignored the heavily built man marching toward them and started down the hall, but Martin pulled him back.

"We're ready to call it a night," Martin said to the guard with a lopsided grin, giving the impression that he might have had too much to drink.

"Did you settle up in there?"

"All settled up and pockets empty," Martin slurred.

"Then go out the way you came in," the man ordered. "That hallway's off-limits."

Martin nodded at Richard to follow. Richard hung back, glaring.

"Don't make a scene," Martin whispered, his face turned away from the guard who stood with his arms folded across a burly chest. The man pointed toward the front exit.

Richard cursed, but followed him. Once outside, Richard flung a fist at him. Martin grabbed his arm and held it. "Watch it. You don't know what you're doing."

"You let him get away. You were too busy with that damn whore," Richard snarled. "We've lost him."

"Listen to me. After what you told me, Harrington either works here or is a regular. He might even own the place. We need to make a plan. You go after him and you'll find out nothing, even be arrested in the process. You don't know his connections or how corrupt the authorities might be. We'll ask questions, find out more about this place, and when we do confront him, he won't have his men around to protect him."

Richard rubbed the back of his neck in frustration. Everything in him wanted to go after Harrington.

"You must know I care deeply for Alaina," Martin said, placing his hand on Richard's shoulder. "I want to find her just as badly as you do. Let me think this through. Right now

Harrington doesn't know that we're after him. And if he didn't want to show his face in the gambling hall, there's a good chance he doesn't want others to know of his connection to the place. That can work in our favor. We'll come back tomorrow night. That girl I was talking to may be just the person to give us the information we need."

"That harlot? How could you be thinking of bedding her when—"

"Stop, Richard, and hear me out. I saw that girl on the street today. She was frightened. She remembered that I had come to her rescue when a man grabbed her."

"So now you're her protector? She was all over you."

"She realized I was English. She whispered to me that she needed help. She came to America with a man who promised her father he would find her respectable work. Instead he brought her here. That's all she had time to tell me. Most likely she'll be punished for not servicing me. I told her I'd help her, but it appears she might be the one to help us."

Richard swore beneath his breath. "I apologize for my mistrust. You have a clearer head than I do."

"Only because my brother and I dealt with the worst in society when we were on the streets. You still have the polish of an aristocrat's son." Martin grinned. "We need to get some rest. I'll be at your hotel in the morning and we'll see what we can accomplish tomorrow."

ALAINA LAY across her bed, fully clothed. Sleep was

useless. She couldn't confront Phillip with what she knew. Once she'd spent every tear at seeing Martin again, she'd pondered every angle over her discovery of Phillip's secret life. She could find no benefit in disclosing what she'd found out about him.

She thought of contacting the men she'd met at the meeting, telling them that her father was dead and the papers they'd been given were forged. But she'd have to speak through the interpreter and she had no idea where to find him. Worse, if she ruined Phillip's chances at closing the trade agreement, she feared what he would do.

She thought of Molly who dreamed of being given a fine position in Boston, better than what she could find in London. And now the poor girl was forced to work as a prostitute.

What would Phillip do to her if she betrayed him?

If she could only find proof of his deception and his forgeries, she might be able to use the evidence against Phillip and save Richard from a conviction. She hadn't been allowed in Phillip's library and the door was kept locked. That thought brought memories back of her father's threats when his privacy was intruded upon. It was as if she were living the same life she'd led under her father's roof.

Maria does the housekeeping. She must have a key. How could she get it without causing suspicion? If Phillip paid a forger, he might have a bill or, if he did his own, some material, copies of signatures, anything that would prove his crime.

Phillip said the contract could be signed this coming week. She didn't have much time. She no longer trusted that he'd burn the false proof he held against Richard. If she found some evidence of his forgery operation, she could try to mail it to Richard. Now that she knew of the forgeries, she was a danger to Phillip. She doubted that he'd allow her to return to London, ever.

If only she could see Martin again and talk to him privately. She might never be able to gain his respect or his love but she knew he would help her.

MARTIN APPEARED at Richard's hotel door at nine the next morning. They ate a light breakfast in the hotel's dining room and discussed their options. Being Sunday, most Bostonians would either be in church or at home. Even the gambling hall would be closed. There was little they could do until later that night.

"I'm going back to the brothel to see that girl," Martin said. "She very well might know Harrington, since he appears to be involved in some way."

"Where do you want to meet? What time?" Richard queried, pushing his chair out as if he were ready to leave at that moment. "Why not go this afternoon? No doubt those girls are plying their trade by then if a man is willing to pay."

"You can't be there, Richard."

"What?" Richard gripped the table edge. "You expect me to stay here and do nothing?"

"Harrington visited you in London. If he recognizes you, he'll know you're searching for your sister. It's too dangerous. He could hide her from us and we'll never find her. Let me go in alone. I'll meet you here later."

"I'll not sit in this hotel, waiting. I won't go in but I'll be there when you come out."

Martin wasn't going to argue with him. He understood his need to be useful. "Just stay out of sight. If you see Harrington, don't confront him. Hopefully, I'll know more once I talk to Molly."

It rained most of the day, causing the streets to flood. Few people were out since even carriages had trouble navigating through the downpour. Martin arrived at the gambling hall, pulling off his soaked slicker once the door closed behind him. He didn't have to search for the madam of the place. Sophie greeted him and remembered him from the night before.

"Well, well, you ain't going to leave my Molly Belle again, are you?" she asked, after Martin handed her the extravagant sum she'd asked for when he told her he desired the girl's company.

"I apologize for my unusual behavior. I realized I drank a bit too much. I didn't want to disappoint her."

Sophie let out a raucous laugh. "My girls' job is to please regardless of how ya perform. Ya might consider Lydie tonight, instead of Molly Belle. She's available and has more experience pleasuring a man such as yourself."

"I like to finish what I start and I prefer the inexperienced ones. She'll be better trained once I have my way with her." Martin curved his lips in a lewd grin.

She acknowledged his meaning with a wink and grin. "Well, if Molly Belle don't satisfy ya, honey, I'd be happy to finish ya off." She brushed her tongue across her bright-red upper lip.

Martin hid his revulsion and followed the woman down the hall to a small room. When he entered, closing the door behind him, he saw Molly sitting on a gaudy flowered spread, her arms wrapped tightly around her folded legs. She wore a scant black negligee that barely hid her nakedness. Her face looked pale and her lips trembled.

Seeing a shawl on a nearby chair, he lifted it and held it up to her. She grabbed it and wrapped it around her, her chin trembling.

He sat at the foot of the small bed, giving the girl space. "Molly, my name is Martin. I want you to tell me how you got into this mess." He watched her as she wiped a tear from her cheek and appeared to relax.

She told him about Phillip Harrington and his promise to her father to find her a position in Boston. "'E wanted me to be a chaperone to 'is fiancée, Miss Alaina, which didn't make much sense after I met her, her bein' older 'en me, but she didn't much like 'im either. I figured it was one of those arranged marriages, but she was nice to me and it was good to 'ave 'er for company."

"You were with Alaina Craymore?" Martin tried to remain calm at the mention of her name and the realization that Molly had spent time with her. He was thankful that Alaina wasn't completely alone, but this girl was no chaperone. He doubted Alaina could have had much in common with her.

"Yes, that was 'er name. I stayed with 'er during the whole journey. Then 'e sent me off in a carriage when we arrived in Boston. 'E told me I was goin' to my new position."

Tears fell as she talked of being brought to the brothel and placed in a room, unable to leave, and Harrington's expectations of her to embrace her new position or expect worse.

"But he is not known as Harrington here, is he?"

"'E talked to me only once when I was locked in the room. Told me if I seen 'im 'ere, never to address 'im by the name 'Arrington, or Phillip, as 'e was called on the ship. If I did, I'd be sorry. I seen 'im a couple o' times talking to Sophie. She called 'im Mr. Cox. I wasn't gonna say anythin' cause I was afraid of 'is threats. 'E said if I disobeyed 'im, 'e'd go back to London and bring my sisters 'ere. They're younger than me."

Martin rubbed the stubble on his chin that he hadn't taken the time to shave off. The man was even more deviant that he'd imagined. "Molly, you've been a great help to me. If you promise not to tell anyone of our conversation, I promise I'll get you out of here as soon as I can."

"But, 'ow? What is it you want?"

"Information and you may have already given me enough."

"If I could just tell Ben," she pleaded. "'E won't tell anyone. 'E wants to get me out o' 'ere too."

"Who is Ben? Tell me about him."

"'E's one of our bodyguards but 'e takes care o' me without Sophie knowin'. We got signals." She lowered her head, hiding her blush. "'E's sweet on me. If Sophie knew 'e'd get fired. If Mr. Harrington ever found out..." Her hand flew to her mouth. "I'm not suppose to ever say 'is name."

Martin absorbed the information. "Are you sure you can trust Ben?"

"Oh, yes. 'E loves me." She smiled for the first time.

Martin wondered if Ben could be another contact in their search for Alaina.

"I may need Ben's help too. If I tell you where he can find me, do you think he'd be willing to seek me out? I could help both of you."

Molly shook her head almost violently. "Yes, I'm sure. 'E don't want to work 'ere anymore but 'e don't want to leave me alone."

Martin gave her his address, told her to mess up the bed and her hair and to crawl under the covers. Deciding that enough time had passed, he left the room, surprised to see the same man who had blocked their way the night before standing near the door. He looked as if he could kill. No one else was around.

"Are you Ben?" Martin asked his voice low and his eyes averted from the man. He wanted no one to notice he was drawing his attention.

Ben looked startled at Martin's question. "Yes, who wants to know?"

Martin nodded toward Molly's door. "Talk to her," he whispered before turning the corner to the front entrance where Sophie sat, apparently waiting for customers.

He gave her a gratifying grin and left before

she could engage him in conversation. Richard had already waited over an hour for him out of view of the entrance. Martin met him a short distance away.

"What did you find out? Does she know where we can find him?"

"Let's walk."

"Tell me you've found something worth hearing."

"Yes, a great deal." Martin told him everything he'd learned from Molly and the identity of the guard who'd directed them to the front exit the night before.

"Do you think either of them can be trusted? The girl's been working as a prostitute and she sounds none too bright. How can you be sure she can keep quiet?"

"She fears for the fate of her younger sisters and she obviously has feelings for the guard. My instincts tell me she'll follow through. If this Ben truly cares for her and wants her out of there, I don't think we'll have to wait very long to hear from him. Most likely he has to work through the night. I expect he'll be at my door when he gets off."

"You sound confident."

"Cautious, yet optimistic. As it is Sunday night, it's the best we have going for us right now."

Chapter Six

RICHARD ARRIVED at Martin's boarding house at seven the next morning. Benjamin Murphy arrived at eight. After introductions, Ben appeared guarded and suspicious.

"What do you want from me and what's your interest in Molly?" he asked, standing inside the door, refusing to take a seat.

"Mr. Murphy. You are aware that she told me of her plight," Martin said, standing eye to eye with the man, while Richard leaned against a nearby wall.

"Yes. Call me Ben. She said you didn't touch her and that you knocked down some swine that put his clammy hands on her in the street."

Ben's expression remained stoic but Martin sensed that he was grateful. "She is a victim of a man who we need to find."

"And what's your business with him?"

"The bastard's got my sister," Richard snarled.

The man turned his head sharply toward Richard. "Your sister?"

"He forced her to come here from London. Every hour we waste standing here, she's in greater danger."

Martin held up a staying hand. Richard looked as if he hadn't slept and his edginess wasn't helping matters.

Ben sneered at Richard. "And every minute my

Molly is in that brothel without me there to protect her, *she* is in danger. So let's get this over with. What do you want from me?"

Martin took a step closer to Ben. "Molly accompanied Richard's sister on the journey from London. Harrington brought them both here for different purposes. Molly's been found, Alaina hasn't. Only Harrington knows where she is. We need to know when Harrington, the man who you call Mr. Cox, arrives at the gaming hall and when he leaves."

"Well, why didn't you say so? We can figure somethin' out."

Within fifteen minutes, they came up with a plan. Martin and Richard would stay in a secluded area outside the gambling hall's front entrance. Ben would signal to them by coming out for a smoke when Harrington arrived. He told them that he usually showed up close to midnight most nights and stayed only a brief time unless he was bedding his favorite whore.

Martin was counting on his arrival tonight.

"He comes in by the back door in the alley," Ben said, "and leaves the same way. No one else is allowed to use that door. That's why I stopped you both when you were heading down that hallway. I can signal you when he arrives, but I don't always know when he leaves. He might be with Brigid or in his back office. I have to be where I'm needed."

Martin nodded in understanding. "Once we know he's in there, you've given us what we want. We'll be waiting for him when he leaves, regardless of the time."

"So I carry through with the plan," Ben said after the men shook hands. "Now, what can you do for Molly?"

"I promise you I will get her out of there as soon as possible."

Ben lowered his head. "Sophie knows I like her. She lets me keep an eye on her and doesn't pass her off to paying patrons who might be rough on her. Problem is, I can't take care of her in Boston," he muttered. "Not without another good-payin' job. She best go back to her family. She'd be harassed here. She ain't no *whore*." Ben twisted his lips in disgust at the word.

"I'll make sure she's returned to her family. I swear that to you," Martin said, feeling compassion for the man.

Ben nodded. He turned and left, shutting the door behind him.

"What do we do now?" Richard asked, staring at the closed door, his expression more embarrassed now than overbearing.

"We will be up most of the night tonight and you look as if that wall is holding you up. Stop punishing yourself with guilt and get a few hours of sleep."

"You must be pleased, Alaina, that the contract has been drawn up. The signing is tomorrow afternoon. You have played your part well and I must say that I've played my cards to perfection. The men are anxious to return to China, making them clay in my hands," he gloated, sitting back in his chair. "You might consider marrying me after all. I am going to be a very wealthy man. You would be a jewel by my side if you could overcome your prudishness. Even your brother might wish to profit. I'd consider him as an associate, if he possesses your father's shrewdness."

Alaina wondered how he could even consider that she or her brother would want any role in his villainy. She hated sitting with him at the dinner table and listening to his arrogance. He'd left for a few hours earlier to meet his clients and had been strutting around the house since learning that the contract was ready to be signed.

While he was gone, she'd tried to carry on a conversation with the housekeeper but it was useless. The woman didn't understand a word of English and she appeared to be afraid to indulge in even an awkward conversation. Still, Alaina had discovered what she wanted. The woman carried house keys in her apron pocket.

Her time was running out, she had to find some evidence that proved forgery. She knew that as soon as the signed contract was in his hands, she was a danger to him.

"I see the news has done nothing to lift your spirits, Alaina. I suggest that you give serious thought to my proposal." He stood and tossed his napkin on the table. "I'll be in my library."

Alaina stayed seated until he left the room, waiting for Lucia to come in to clear the dishes.

"May I help?" Alaina didn't wait for the woman to wave her away as she usually did. She picked up her dish and silverware and carried them to the kitchen. Lucia scurried after her, bellowing in her native tongue. Alaina knew despite the language difference that the woman was pleading with her not to take on her duties.

Once in the kitchen, Alaina pointed to the dining room, letting the woman know that she expected her to continue clearing the table. When Lucia reluctantly left the kitchen, she hurried to the pantry where aprons hung on hooks. She checked the pockets of each one, sighing with relief when one of them held a set of keys. She returned to the kitchen just as Lucia returned, carrying platters from the table.

Alaina offered a smile and left the room. The poor woman looked mystified at her odd behavior. Lucia's inability to speak English was in her favor. She knew she would say nothing to Phillip. She ran up the stairs to her bedroom and shut the door. Pulling the keys from her pocket, she examined each one, praying that Phillip would leave tonight for the gambling hall and that one of the keys would open the library door.

PHILLIP LOCKED the library door after entering and closing it behind him. He had to make a plan for his future now that he was finally closing the deal. The contract was in order and signing was the final technicality. The men would be on a ship the following morning.

He walked to his desk, still in awe that he'd accomplished what had appeared to be impossible. Despite Craymore's death and his son's stupidity, he'd succeeded. He'd played on Alaina's weakness and won. Now he needed to get rid of all evidence of his illegal occupations.

He reached under his desk chair for the key to his hidden sanctuary. Closing off a section of his office for a storage area had allowed him the ideal space for his small but profitable operation. He walked the few feet to what he privately called his forger's closet and unlocked the door. Looking around at the papers and tools of his covert trade, he considered how best to get rid of everything. He no longer needed any of it and his mind would be free of the fear of being discovered.

He'd separate himself from the gambling hall and brothel as well. He needed none of it anymore. He'd be a member of the elite of Boston. He might even consider running for an office.

He lifted papers strewn on the table before him and smirked at the signature samples, the falsified documents and the blank bank notes. Grabbing a handful of the evidence, he tossed them into the cinder bucket he used to carry trash to the fireplace. When he returned tonight, he'd begin the burning.

The only documents he'd hold on to were those with Richard's signature. His dear sister had thrown away her reputation for him. Why would she even want to return to England and face society's scorn? He would try again to convince her that it was worth her while to marry him.

He was tired of his covert activities. He wanted respectability and admiration from men of privilege, even the snobs who had previously ignored him. They would desire his attention.

He'd be a changed man. If he convinced Alaina to marry him, his voluptuous Brigid would still be available to service his needs. If the promise of vast wealth wouldn't alter Alaina Craymore's conscience, perhaps the threat of life in a brothel might.

ALAINA HAD waited too long already. Phillip had been gone for some time but it had taken her that long to gather her courage. She set down her candle on the floor next to the library door and tried one key and then another, her hands trembling. When she heard the click of the lock, she let out the breath she'd been holding for too long.

She entered the library, set down the candle and closed the door. Looking around the room, she was surprised to see that it was smaller than expected and L-shaped. Walking around Phillip's desk to the back corner, she spotted another door that led to an enclosed space.

It appeared that a section of the room had been walled off. Was it used as a closet or a storage room? The door to the room was locked. She tried one key and then another, but none of them opened it.

The housekeeper mustn't be allowed in there.

She went to his desk, opened each drawer, fingering their contents, nothing was worthy of her attention. She searched throughout the room, turning up nothing and time was slipping away. *He must have a key to that room hidden somewhere.* She returned to the desk and rummaged through the drawers again. Feeling frantic and careless, she hoped she'd returned everything to its proper place. *What if he realizes that I've been in here?* She couldn't dwell on the consequences.

She continued her search, finally getting down on her knees looking under the desk and the chair. There, she'd spotted it, a key hanging from a small hook and hidden well under the chair's wood and upholstery. She dislodged it and gripped it in her hands. Pulling herself up, she ran to the locked door. The key turned easily in the lock.

Opening the door, she stared into the darkness. She hurried back for the candle and held it in front of her as she entered the small space. She stood amazed at her discovery. Various sizes of paper, inkwells and pens sat on shelves. On a large flat table before her were stacks of documents. A cinder bucket left beside the table held torn and wrinkled sheets of paper. She lifted one and then another and found samples of signatures penned on the papers, some were smudged but they left no doubt they were discarded attempts at forgery, tossed in the bucket to be burned.

She browsed through the stacks of paper on the table that included a variety of documents, bank notes, letters and containers of sealing wax. Her heart raced in her chest. Here was all the proof she needed. She shuffled through the stacks, looking for familiar documents like the ones that carried her father's or brother's names.

Perhaps they'd already been burned.

She pulled wrinkled papers from the cinder bucket and took copies from the stacks on the table that appeared official and letters that held signatures. When she lifted the final stack, she saw her father's signature. She pulled it from the rest.

She looked again, hoping to find her brother's signature, but without any luck. Disappointed but satisfied that no one could doubt Phillip's crime, she straightened the piles and left, locking the door and returning the key to its hiding place.

She took a final look around the library to see if anything appeared out of place. Carrying the candle in one hand and the stack of papers pressed to her breast, she left the room. She fidgeted for the keys she'd tucked in a pocket, found the right one and locked the door. Remaining vigilant, she walked quietly to the stairs. She was nearly to the top when she heard the twist of the front doorknob. She gasped and hurried up the remaining stairs and flew through the upper corridor to her room. Rushing inside, she nearly dropped the candle, her hands shook so badly. She listened for footsteps, but heard nothing. She sucked in a breath. A minute longer and he would have found her.

She set the candle down on her night table, reached under her bed and pulled out her traveling satchel. After stuffing the papers inside, she pushed it beneath the bed.

She sunk down on the coverlet. Phillip hadn't come upstairs. He must have gone to his library. What if he discovered something amiss? She shuddered at the thought.

She didn't move, listening and waiting for him to climb the stairs. She wanted to hear his bedroom door close, but there was only silence.

As the time passed, her eyes grew heavy from lack of sleep. She shook her head to ward off her drowsiness. "Oh, no." She jumped up from the bed.

The keys. She pulled them from her pocket.

She looked toward the window. It would be dawn soon and Maria would be arriving to begin her morning chores. What would she do if she found them missing? Would she go to the library, seeking Phillip out and pointing to the empty pocket of her apron? She pictured him tearing up the stairs looking for her, accusing her.

She went to the door, opened it slowly and peered out. She stepped into the hallway. She had no choice, the keys had to be returned before Maria discovered them missing.

BEN GAVE his signal just after midnight. Martin and Richard both stared at each other, relieved that the past two hours waiting had not been in vain. They made their way around the corner and to the opposite side of the street where they could observe the alleyway and prepare themselves for another long wait. When Harrington finally emerged over two hours later, they followed a good distance behind him until he turned a corner.

When they reached the corner, they saw Harrington enter a tavern.

"Damn, it looks like he's stopping for a drink. I'm going in after him." Richard bolted forward.

Martin grabbed his coat, pulling him back. He wished he could handle this himself without having to constantly curb Richard's rage. "Use your head, man. We may never find out where Alaina is if we go bounding in there. Let him have his drinks. We'll wait until he leaves. If he doesn't lead us to her, then we'll grab him when he's alone and force the truth out of him."

Another hour passed before Harrington stepped out of the tavern. They followed him for a few more blocks until he arrived at a brownstone. They watched as he climbed the steps, entered and closed the door behind him.

"My sister might be in there. We have to find out."

"Wait," Martin warned, raising a hand to quiet him. "You are not the only one who wants her safe, but rushing in is not practical."

Richard balled his fists. "What do you expect me to do? She thought she was protecting me. She has sacrificed her reputation for nothing."

"Worthy reasons, but foolish actions," Martin muttered, as he walked cautiously to the side of the building and stared up at the second-floor windows.

"Since you seem able to remain so composed, what do you suggest we do?"

"Composed?" Martin frowned. "Do not doubt that I want to go in there and rip the man apart and leave him for the dogs. York and I faced too many situations where reactions created more problems. Close observation sometimes reveals more than rash action." As he spoke, he kept eyeing the rooms above him. "Look up at those windows."

"What is it, what do you see?"

Martin pointed to an upstairs window near the front of the building. "Most likely bedrooms are up there. See that candle flickering in the front room? The window in the rear is dark. Let's see if anything changes. Give him a short time to settle in. I'm going to walk around to the rear and check out the back entrance. Keep an eye out."

Martin walked to the back and checked the door. It was locked but he knew he'd have no problem getting it open.

When he returned to Richard's side, he followed his gaze up toward the roof. Smoke that hadn't appeared before was billowing out of a chimney.

"Harrington must be feeding a fire with more than wood," Richard said. "Look at those cinders flying about."

"He looked like he'd had more than a couple of drinks, I thought he'd be passed out by now."

"There is still only a flicker of a candle in the upstairs room and the other remains dark. Harrington must have remained on the first floor, perhaps, feeding a fire in a study or a parlor," Martin mused. "I am going in there, now," he said, keeping his voice even.

"Let's go."

"I am going in alone."

"No!"

"Do I need to remind you that I've had a little practice in breaking and entering? I know what I'm doing and I need you to wait here."

Richard opened his mouth to protest, but Martin raised a hand to stop him.

"Let me investigate. Two of us might cause a disturbance. Trust me, Richard."

ALAINA MADE her way down the hallway, passing Phillip's closed bedroom door. She wanted to use the back stairs, which were closest to the kitchen. Lucia was most likely still asleep, though she suspected she'd be up making breakfast soon. She walked silently down the stairs, the keys gripped tightly in her hand.

When she reached the bottom step, an arm went about her waist and a hand covered her mouth.

Phillip. She tried to force out a scream but the hand pressed harder against her lips. She struggled until she heard a familiar voice—it wasn't Phillip's.

"*Ssshh.*" The floor beneath her seemed to sway and disappear when he turned her around and in the dim light of predawn, she saw Martin's face. He slowly uncovered her mouth.

"Alaina," Martin murmured before his tone grew into a huskier, harsher whisper. "What the hell are you doing here? Come, we are getting out of here now." He grabbed her arm and pulled her through the back door.

A rush of cool night air cleared Alaina's head as Martin nearly dragged her out the back door and around the house where Richard stood.

"Alaina, thank God," Richard pulled her to him.

Alaina caught her breath and looked into her brother's eyes. Everything was happening too fast. She barely had her footing. "I can't believe you found me," her voice quavered.

"You're safe now," Richard said, wrapping his arms around her.

"I need to go back." She remembered the evidence she'd taken. She couldn't leave it behind and she still had the keys in her hand.

"You'll not stay under that man's roof one more hour," Richard snapped.

She pulled free from her brother's grasp and turned to Martin.

"I found evidence to prove my brother's innocence. I can't leave it here."

She saw the stubborn set of Martin's jaw, but she could be just as stalwart. She hadn't gone through all of this only to have failed in saving her brother. She turned to Richard. "Phillip is a forger. I have proof of it. He might destroy it if we leave it behind. Please listen…"

"Tell me where it is. I'll find it," Martin interrupted her. "And both of you keep your voices down. Alaina, you are going with your brother."

"Martin, you have done enough," Richard whispered. "Let me go in there this time. You were right all along. We might never have found her if I'd had my way, but she is safe now."

Martin stood his ground, refusing to move. "I am the only one going back in there. Get Alaina to safety."

"I'll not let you put yourself in danger again. This is my problem."

Alaina, freed from her brother's grasp as the men argued, bolted and headed for the back door. Martin caught her just she reached the entrance.

"Like I said, you are not going back in there. Tell me what I should be looking for. We are wasting precious time."

She sighed heavily. "In the satchel under my bed. I can show you."

"Is your bedroom upstairs in the front of the house?"

She looked at him and nodded. How did he know?

He seemed to read her mind. "I saw a candle flickering. Obviously, you were still awake or you wouldn't have been roaming around the house in the early-morning hours. *Phillip*, as you called him, had just arrived home."

He appeared angry but she had no time to explain her exploits.

"Go back to your brother. I'll find your evidence and take care of Harrington. Go!"

She looked into his eyes, saw his determination, and walked away. When she looked back, Martin had disappeared into the house that had been her prison.

ALAINA WOKE to the sound of voices in Richard's adjoining room. Hurrying from the bed to the closed door, she hesitated, opened it a crack and listened.

"I need to get her on a ship back to England, away from Harrington's clutches," Richard said, his voice low to Martin.

"I understand. I'll make arrangements for your travel."

"No, Martin, I'll go to the docks this morning and take care of it." They obviously thought she was still asleep, Alaina thought. She remained where she was as she watched them, thankful that Martin was here and safe, but irritated at the way they were planning her return without her input.

She frowned when she looked down at the gown she'd slept in. Using her fingers as a comb, she brushed at her wayward curls. Still, she didn't open the door fully and make her presence known. How could she face Martin? He'd saved her from Harrington, but he couldn't save her from her disgrace.

Alaina breathed a sigh of relief when she saw her satchel open on the chair near where Martin stood and papers in her brother's hands.

"We need to bring these to the authorities too," her brother said.

"Not so fast," Martin said. "I'll take care of that. I also need to keep my promise to Molly. If it wasn't for her help, we wouldn't have found Alaina."

"To think that Harrington forced her into prostitution after using her to accompany my sister."

Alaina lowered her eyes, remembering Molly at the gambling hall. She had helped Martin find her and she'd thought that the girl wanted only his attentions.

"I'll pay for a chaperone to accompany my sister back to London. I can't let you finish this dirty business alone."

"*No.*" Alaina pulled open the door. "You'll not send me back while you stay here, Richard. I'll only continue to worry about you. We need to see him arrested."

"Alaina   is   partially   correct," Martin interrupted. "You need to accompany her. If she must go back, she'll need your support when she faces the dragons of society. I will take care of Harrington. He will never bother either of you again."

"This is not your problem," Richard barked. "You have helped us enough."

Martin frowned, appearing impatient. "You have no idea what men Harrington has in his pocket. Corruption is as prevalent here as it is in London. Leave the man to me. He'll not cause anyone harm again once I'm through with him. You need to hold on to some of this evidence and bring it to your lawyers in London as soon as you arrive. There is no more you can do here."

Alaina cringed. *Oh, heavens, what a horrid mess I've made.*

Martin turned to Alaina. "I can only imagine the worry that Lady Henley and my sister-in-law are going through. I suppose you need to get back as soon as possible to ease their minds."

Suppose? What an odd word to use, she thought, but what could she say to that? She knew that Cornelia and Marielle feared for her safety and surely Martin must want her out of his sight after her shameful actions. Yet his words were a contradiction—it was almost as if he wished to present an alternative, ask her to stay.

Martin interrupted her thoughts. "I need to ask you, do you remember the names of any of Harrington's business associates? That would be helpful."

"Yes, I remember names and the hotel where we met the men from China." She proceeded to tell them both about the trade deal and the contract to be signed that day. When she finished, she could see that Richard looked astonished and Martin appeared both pleased and disturbed at her knowledge and the situation.

"Your attention to detail will make my objectives easier, Alaina," Martin said finally.

Because of her actions, Martin was placing himself in danger. What would Phillip do to anyone who got in his way today? she wondered.

"Martin, how can I help?" Richard asked.

"You can help by assuring Alaina's safety right now. There is absolutely nothing you could do but get these papers to your lawyers. Forgive my frankness, Richard, but York and I dealt with criminals worse than Harrington. You will only be in the way of my efforts."

Richard nodded in resignation. He looked at his sister. "We need to get you some traveling clothes and get to the docks to make reservations. I'm going to pack my things in case we find passage. Get ready to leave." He clasped Martin's arm in wordless appreciation, turned and walked into his bedroom, leaving the door open.

Alaina didn't move, ignoring her brother's order.

"You should listen to your brother," Martin murmured.

Alaina stared at him. She wanted to say something, to explain, but her shame silenced her. Her reasons hardly mattered, she had compromised her virtue. What must he be thinking of her?

Martin went to the window and looked down

at the street below. She watched in silence. His hair was longer and though he'd tied it back, loose strands fell carelessly. He was more ruggedly handsome then she remembered, his complexion swarthier, the shadow of a beard making him appear older. Though he'd never really looked the part of a polished aristocrat, he seemed even rougher around the edges, yet more self-assured.

"Martin, I can only imagine what you must be thinking. I feared that Richard would be imprisoned. I thought of your father…" She bit her lip when his head snapped back at the mention of Lord Blackstone. How she wished she hadn't said that. She could see his face grimace at her words. "I only meant—"

"You needn't explain." Martin turned around, reached out and touched her cheek.

She hadn't expected a tender touch or the look of pity she saw in his piercing gray eyes. She caught herself, straightened her back and stiffened her chin. She wanted his love, not his pity. She had brought ruin upon herself and now she must pay the price.

She followed his gaze as he looked toward Richard who was tossing his clothes in a suitcase, his back partially hidden by the half-closed door. He pulled her toward him. "Damn, Alaina, how could you put yourself in such danger?" he whispered gruffly. "Do you have any idea what you've done to yourself, to those who care about you?"

She cast her eyes down, unable to look at him.

He grasped a handful of mahogany curls

hanging down her back and tugged until her face lifted to his, his lips only inches from hers. "I was right here, in Boston, buying horses. I have bought land. I was making plans, creating a future."

He loosened his hold and dropped his hands to her shoulders. "You were here all along—with him." His face twisted in a mixture of anger and pain. "I thought leaving was for the best. You needed time to mourn your loss, I needed..." He let her go, stepped back. "Why in God's name didn't you talk to someone? Was there no other way?"

Alaina reached out to a nearby chair to steady herself. He hadn't accepted her explanation and he blamed her. He abhorred her for what she'd done, what she had become.

"I couldn't tell anyone. I didn't know what else to do."

Martin's face softened. He gripped her arms, his eyes darting toward the bedroom once again before returning to her gaze. "Alaina, stay in America," he said in an almost gentle voice. "If you return to England, you'll be treated as an outcast. We'll marry. No one will scorn you here under my protection. You deserve better than the disgrace you'll face at home."

Alaina's mouth dropped open before she stepped back, understanding his sacrifice, while her insides raged at the irony. *He'd marry me, fulfill the desires of my heart...out of pity, to save my reputation.*

Martin tried to draw her back, his hands clenching her tighter. "I'll talk to your brother. He needs to know that you'll be safe until I take care of

Harrington. I'll figure something out." He seemed to be thinking out loud. "I told that girl, Molly, I'd get her back to her family. Richard could return her there. It'll work out. You won't have to face any contempt. I owe you that for leaving England without a word to you, after our intimacy. I was wrong, Alaina."

"You owe me nothing," Alaina breathed out, holding back tears and wanting to escape the pain that coursed through her. He spoke no words of love or affection, only contrition. *He believes he compromised me with a kiss, a kiss that meant nothing more to him than a flirtation.* She had ignored the truth for too long; instead, held on to a dream. If she'd meant more to him, he wouldn't have left without a pledge to return to her.

"My brother and I owe you much," she said through thinned lips, her head held higher. "You have taken on too much responsibility for us already. No, I shall return to England and face whatever I must." She could hardly believe what she was saying. The man she loved offered her marriage. She could spend the rest of her life with him, loving him. But, she couldn't allow him to sacrifice his future to save her from disgrace. He pitied her and he would never forget that she'd compromised her reputation. No, he'd done enough.

The truth, as painful as it was, caused her to push away from him. She'd rather face humiliation and scorn than accept his sacrificial offer.

Before more could be said, Richard walked through the door.

"Are you ready, Alaina?"

"I need a few minutes." She looked at Martin for the last time, then turned abruptly and walked back into her room, shutting the door behind her.

WHERE HAD he gone wrong? He'd offered to marry her. He'd apologized for leaving without a word to her. Martin went over the entire scenario in his mind as he rode toward Harrington's house. His mind should be on his plan, but he couldn't erase Alaina's cold response to his proposal. *Doesn't she realize that the ton will grind her to the ground with their gossip and cruel judgments?* He must convince her to stay.

Richard would be making arrangements this morning and most likely, they would have to wait at least a day if not more for a ship prepared to leave for Liverpool. When he finished what he needed to do, he'd go back to the hotel and talk to her, make her understand that he wanted her to stay with him.

Now he had to focus on Harrington.

He'd already thought of all kinds of torture he would like to personally administer to the scoundrel. The consequences of rash action, however, could foil his plans. If he was jailed, how could he protect Alaina if he talked her into staying?

The reality that she'd been in Boston and in danger while he was going about his business still enraged him. He'd thought that she was safely in the care of Lady Henley, healing and, he'd hoped, waiting for his return.

He had to make it up to her. If she insisted on going back to England, he would finish his business and get on a ship as soon as possible. She'd have already been subject to the wrath of society and be more open to listening to him. He would save her reputation, marry her, and if she didn't want to return to America with him, then he would stay in England. No harm would ever come to her again.

For now he might have to accept her return to England. Until Harrington was taken care of, she could still be in danger. He'd try to talk some sense into her tonight if Harrington was no longer an issue. He'd have to figure it out later. He would truly think of her needs, not his own.

He rode by horseback to Harrington's house after making a couple of stops. Alaina had furnished him with names of men in business and he knew where they were located. His first stop was the hotel where the men from China were staying. Since it was still early morning, he left messages for them, briefly explaining Harrington's deception, describing the proof of his forgery, which, he wrote, would be handed over to officials. Finally, he left the address of his brothel, disclosed his alias and his urging for the men to visit for further proof.

Since Harrington had arrived home in the early-morning hours, Martin was hoping that he was asleep and unaware of Alaina's disappearance, unless the man made a habit of visiting her in her bedroom. The thought sickened him. He couldn't ask Alaina if Harrington had taken advantage of her. The truth was he didn't want to know.

Once he was satisfied with the scoundrel's demise, he needed to travel to Virginia, make arrangements with his overseer concerning his land and livestock and return to Boston for Molly. Having learned that the girl was brought to America with Alaina under false pretenses and forced into prostitution, he couldn't leave her at the brothel. He would take her back to England with him and return her to her family.

He arrived at Harrington's apartment and let himself in the same way he had the previous night. It was a sunless morning that promised rain and early enough for Harrington to be asleep after a night of heavy drinking. He listened for the sounds of a servant milling about but at least the hallway was quiet. He padded quietly up the stairs and entered Harrington's bedroom without a sound. Sure enough, he was snoring, his face half buried in his pillow, one arm hanging off the side of the bed. His clothes from the night before were strewn haphazardly on the floor.

Martin crept softly to a corner chair, pulled out his pistol, and sat glaring in revulsion at the tyrant. For a brief moment, he considered slamming Harrington on the head, setting fire to the room and walking out, but just as he savored the thought Harrington began to stir. Martin waited, polishing the metal of his pistol with his handkerchief. He watched as Harrington stretched on his back, rubbed his eyes and snorted loudly, before pushing off his covers and swinging his legs over the side of the bed. His feet had barely touched the floor when he saw Martin, his eyes drawing immediately to the pistol aimed at his most vulnerable area.

"What the hell? Who are you? What are you doing in here?" Harrington growled as his hands hovered protectively over his groin.

Martin, steely eyed, grinned, his rage contained.

"Perhaps you might ask Miss Craymore who I am, though you would have a difficult time finding her. She and her brother are preparing to board a ship back to England."

Harrington's eyes grew wide. Martin sneered when he saw the look of confusion and fear that swept over the man's features.

"I demand that you tell me who you are and what the hell you're talking about," Harrington sputtered.

"I'd prefer not to waste my time. To keep it simple, Harrington, your ploy to use the Craymore name to your advantage has exploded in your face." Martin lifted the gun and moved it in a circular motion, stopped and aimed the barrel directly at Harrington's eyes.

Reacting instantly, Harrington threw his arms across his face and ducked into the bed sheets.

Martin laughed at his cowardice and waited while he slowly lifted his head and looked up, terror embedded in his features.

The man was pitiful, Martin thought, as he watched him squirm, the kind of man who attempted to scam with his words but had no backbone. Martin stood and walked over to the bed and spoke in measured words. "Before this day is out, you miserable worm, the men you have attempted to scam will be making a fool of you — that is, after I'm through with you. In fact, by now they should be opening the letters I dropped off this morning, detailing your charade." Martin smiled as Harrington's face distorted into disbelief and panic.

He tried to stand but when Martin took a step closer, he shrank back, his feet lifting from the floor, the action folding him into a near-fetal position. The man was a simpering coward. Humiliation was the best punishment for him. "Get dressed. You and I have some business to take care of."

"Listen, please, whoever you are..." Harrington sat up, opening his hands in a gesture of appeal. "You are being misled." His posture straightened and his voice gained strength as he went on. "I am merely closing a business deal begun by Miss Craymore's father. She agreed to protect both her and her brother's interests. If you'll let me explain, you could benefit financially. But if something happens to me, Richard Craymore —"

"If something happens to you, the world will be a much better place," Martin interrupted, pointing the gun into Harrington's upturned face. "Richard Craymore knows of your forgeries. Is that your usual method of thievery, to manufacture evidence to exploit your victims?"

"You have no proof of forgery."

"But we do." Martin grinned. "We have papers that prove you are a forger."

"That's impossible. I've burned —"

Martin laughed. "Was that what you were doing when you arrived home earlier? We saw all the sparks from your chimney. The problem is, Alaina had already found your hiding place and provided us with all the proof needed to drown you in your own vices."

Harrington sucked in a breath. "You could benefit..." Harrington stopped as the nose of the gun brushed his sweat-beaded forehead.

"Using Alaina Craymore was your biggest mistake," Martin snapped. The desire to blast a hole in the snake was becoming irresistible. "Get your britches on, now, unless you want to walk out of here in your nightclothes and make a bigger fool of yourself."

Harrington's hands shook as he dressed. As he bent down to pull on his boots he glanced at Martin. As Harrington shoved his hand beneath the mattress, Martin brought his fist down and slammed the butt of his gun across his face while he used his free hand to punch Harrington in the gut. The gun Harrington had hidden beneath the mattress clattered to the floor.

Harrington moaned and choked before spitting out blood along with two teeth.

Martin pulled back and balled his fists to regain control. He wanted to finish him but leaving him in the hands of the men he wanted to scam was a smarter option. He glared down at Harrington. "You have finally shown some mettle. Try anything like that again and I will break both your legs. Now finish putting on those damn boots and let's get out of here."

Harrington grabbed the sheet to wipe the blood from his face before putting on the last boot while Martin waited at the door.

"Where are you taking me?" Harrington grunted as he stumbled past Martin and out the door.

"To visit your friendly neighborhood brothel, Mr. Cox. We shall use your carriage."

Harrington's bloody mouth dropped open.

"That's right, Cox. I have visited your establishment."

Harrington remained silent, his face ashen, blood dripping from his nose.

"You are the one who will pay. When we get there, you will tell your manager, Sophie, isn't it? You will tell her that Molly, the girl you have terrorized, will be coming with me. I suggest that you tell the other ladies there to find different employment as well. News of your crimes will spread. In fact, it will be fortunate for you if you get out of Boston alive."

Only a few kicks and shoves were needed to lead Harrington out to the yard and into the carriage. With his gun hidden beneath his coat, Martin ordered him to take the reins and ride to the gambling hall.

When they arrived, Sophie and a couple of the girls were sitting drinking coffee in the front parlor. They looked up in shock at the intrusion.

"Mr. Cox, what happened to ya?" Sophie asked, her mouth remaining open when Martin pushed him into the room.

"None of your business." Harrington shot a

look at the two women who were glaring at him. "Get out of here."

"Do what he says," Sophie ordered, looking fearful.

Martin pointed to a nearby chair. "Sit down, Cox. Sophie, where does he keep the week's proceeds?"

"How dare you!" Harrington hissed.

"I want you to get the cashbox and bring it here. Have your girls line up in the hall. You're going to divide it up between them and send them on their way. Bring Molly in here."

Sophie didn't move, looking confused, until Martin waved the gun he held toward the door. She scuttled out.

"I want to know your name," Harrington spat out.

"You have no need to know, only to remember that I know yours."

Sophie returned with the cashbox and Molly. Once the money was counted and divided up among the other girls, Martin sent them on their way. Molly stood to the side, looking frightened. He handed her a share of the profits just as a guard charged into the room and leaped toward Martin, pushing him to the ground and stepping on his gun hand until Martin released his hold. The man pushed it aside.

"Mr. Cox, you all right?"

"It took you long enough to get in here, Godfrey." Harrington brushed the sleeves of his coat. "Tie him up and, Sophie, lock that bitch in her room." He pointed to Molly who was crouching in a corner.

The man pulled Martin to his feet and twisted his arms back. Even Martin's large build couldn't compare to this giant, who looked as mean as he was huge.

"You're the one who's going to pay," Harrington spit out.

Martin refused to take his eyes off Harrington.

"Lock him up in the basement," Harrington ordered.

He sneered as the guard pushed Martin through the doors only to be pushed back into the room. A fist jammed into the man's face before Martin could see who had done the damage. Ben appeared and grabbed Martin's aggressor by the collar. Harrington squirmed out of the way, trying to reach Martin's gun that had been tossed across the floor. Martin got there first.

He shot it in the air, causing the guards to stop the scuffling. Ben pushed the other man to the floor. "Godfrey, you're helpin' the wrong man."

"Nice to see you again, Ben," Martin said, nodding his gratitude. "You might need to tie your friend up."

"Godfrey will protect whoever pays him."

Martin took a good look at the giant who appeared dimwitted and was now pressed against the wall. "Godfrey, your boss here has no money left to pay you. Isn't that right, Sophie?"

Sophie, who held the empty cashbox, opened it.

"I'll give you a week's wages, Godfrey, if the two of you can help Sophie here."

Martin pushed Harrington until he tripped over a chair and landed on the floor. "Remove Mr. Cox's boots and britches."

"What? Are you mad?" Harrington barked as he scrambled into a nearby corner.

Martin merely waved the men over, each of them pulling off one of Harrington's boots.

"Now his britches."

The men tugged at his trousers, pulling them down over his knees and struggling to yank them off each leg while Harrington fought for purchase.

"Now, Miss Sophie, go find something to tie him up," Martin ordered. He grabbed the dollars that remained on the table, Sophie's share. "I'll give you yours when you get back, that is if you hurry."

Sophie returned within five minutes with ropes and straps. Martin realized they must have been easily accessible since they appeared to be tools of the trade.

"Some men will be looking for your boss shortly. I want him to be ready to receive them." After binding Harrington, he handed Godfrey and Ben money from his own pocket and sent Sophie on her way. He checked the time. He had no doubt that Harrington's associates wouldn't be far behind.

Assured that there was no one else in the building except Ben, he told him to expect visitors and urged him to restrain himself from wrapping his large hands around Harrington's neck.

He led Molly out and just as he was about to latch the carriage door with her safely inside, two well-dressed men on horseback rode around the corner and came to a halt before the entrance. They were off their horses in no time and appeared in a rage.

"Are you looking for Phillip Harrington?" Martin asked as he climbed into the driver's seat.

One of them nodded, the others had murder on their faces.

"He's tied up at the moment in the front room. You might want to address him as Mr. Cox." He saluted them and drove off.

Once Molly was in the care of his landlady, Mrs. Riley, he'd finish this nasty business, find Alaina before she boarded a ship and convince her to stay in America.

Chapter Seven

ALAINA GLANCED about her stateroom, her body taut, her lips tightly pressed together as tears threatened. She would not cry. A welcomed numbness had crept in after the ship had left the dock and as if she were walking in her sleep, she found her way to her stateroom, thankful to be alone. Richard had chosen to stay on deck. She couldn't bear to watch the receding land, knowing that Martin remained and her dreams of spending her life with him were shattered forever.

He could never look at her again as he did on the Blackstone balcony which seemed ages ago. She had no doubt that he had lost respect for her and had offered marriage out of pity. She appreciated his gallantry and he would have saved her once again, this time from humiliation and disgrace. But it was not enough for her. She wanted his love. Refusing his proposal was the only decision she'd made in a long time that she felt at peace about. She wouldn't let him sacrifice his life to save her reputation. He'd done enough.

Their final moments together were tense and too abrupt. He'd insisted that he would finish the business with Harrington and refused their help. Though she knew Martin's past had prepared him to handle the worst of situations, she would wonder and worry until they received news from him of the outcome.

Trying to push aside thoughts of him, she forced herself to open the small traveling chest Richard had purchased for her and unpack the hurriedly bought clothing that would suffice on the voyage back to England. They hadn't expected to be on a ship so soon. When they'd reached the docks to inquire about passage, they found that a ship was preparing to leave in a few hours. Richard was able to obtain passage for a hefty fee. The remaining hours until the ship left port were a blur as they purchased needed items and boarded the ship just before the captain gave the orders to set sail.

She'd had no time to think, but now that she was alone in her stateroom, memories of the past few weeks flooded her mind. The relief she felt at being freed from Harrington's grasp was overshadowed by haunting guilt and shame. She'd lived in deception, a fake, an imposter. She hardly knew who she was anymore. How could she vanquish the memories? She could not have imagined that she would have been capable of her actions and behaviors over the past few weeks. Yet she was on her way back to a life of manners and decorum.

She pulled out one simple gown and then another to be worn at dinners with the captain. She hung them up mechanically and set a pair of shoes beneath them. She pulled open a drawer and filled it with the necessary undergarments and pushed it closed. Finding a shawl, she wrapped it about her shoulders, feeling suddenly cold.

Her thoughts went to her brother who'd grown

silent once they were on board. She knew he had struggled with honoring Martin's demands to leave Harrington to him, but Richard had placed her protection above his own desires. What could she say to him? She understood his frustration but felt too much self-incrimination herself to offer him support. They were on their way home while Martin was left to clean up the mess she'd made.

Her nightmare with Harrington was over and when she arrived in London, she'd be facing a different kind of nightmare, the scathing mouths of the ton. Richard had told her of Cornelia and Marielle's scheme to keep her absence a secret by claiming she was spending time in the country. This news left her feeling even worse. Her dearest friends felt compelled to become involved with deception for her sake. She doubted that the ruse would succeed and worse, it was wrong. She deserved disgrace and they were putting their own reputations at risk for her. How could she repay their kindness?

A sudden change in the ship's movement caused her to stumble. She grasped the bed rail and sat on the edge of the bunk. She remembered the change from her earlier voyage. They had reached open sea, heading toward home. If anything, she could be thankful for the long voyage. She needed time to prepare for a future she had no desire to face.

MARTIN SWORE as he marched out of the hotel where Richard had lodged. They were gone and would not return. According to the hotel manager,

Richard had paid his bill and told him that they'd found a ship that was leaving today. He'd never expected that they'd find passage so soon.

Tomorrow, but not today.

He needed to see Alaina again, to beg her to stay with him.

He'd spent the last couple of hours getting Molly settled and planning his words to convince Alaina that it was in her best interest to marry him. With all that had transpired this morning and Harrington taken care of, he could keep her safe and protect her from society's scorn.

Maybe it wasn't too late.

He mounted his horse and rode swiftly to the docks. It was only a short distance. Perhaps the ship hadn't left port. He ignored the angry looks of pedestrians as his horse's hooves tore up dirt and mud in his rush to find them. When he arrived, he saw a crowd of people leaving and going off in different directions. It wasn't a good sign. They'd most likely been seeing family and friends off and returning to their own homes.

He swore when he looked out into the harbor. He didn't have to dismount. He could see the ship in the distance, its sails being drawn up, preparing for the open sea. His heart grew heavy in his chest as he sat rigid in his saddle and watched the ship grow smaller in the distance. He nodded his head slowly, trying to accept a reality his mind refused to absorb.

He felt scourged with a loneliness unlike anything he'd felt before. He'd dreamed of her all the time they'd been apart and when he'd learned of her victimization, he'd become single minded in his need to find her. The act of removing her from Harrington's grasp, he had carried out with the confidence he had in himself to overcome harrowing circumstances.

His inner turmoil was much more difficult to overcome. His heart had twisted in fear for her safety and seeing her again had ignited a passion within him that only she could temper.

And now she was gone and this time, she'd left him. She had refused him, more willing to face the shame of society than to stay with him. His desire to see Alaina again had been realized, only to lose her again.

Once the ship had disappeared beyond the horizon, he pulled at his horse's reins and started back to his boarding house, feeling tired and defeated.

As he rode, anger took the place of his despondency. He had blundered the proposal, offered it in haste, and without the right words. He'd never told her how much she meant to him, that he'd dreamed of her almost nightly since he'd arrived in America, that in everything he was doing on his plantation in Virginia, his mind was considering their future, not his alone.

He had to go after her.

He thought of all he needed to do before he could board a ship back to England. Though he'd promised to return Molly to her parents, he might have to find her a traveling companion if she wanted to return immediately. He had to finish his business here, inform his land steward of his departure and settle accounts. He had no idea how long he'd be in England. He wouldn't take another refusal from Alaina. He'd stay until she realized that they were meant to be together and if she agreed to marry him but desired to stay in England, then he wouldn't return. He'd sell the land and do his best to conform to a proper Englishman if that's what Alaina wanted. Despite his love of his land and the freedom he felt in America, it meant nothing without her.

He thought of the treatment Alaina would no doubt receive once she was back in London and his hands tightened on the reins. He growled at the thought of the inevitable contempt and ridicule awaiting her that she did not deserve. Worse, that she'd stiffened her spine and chosen to face ruin rather than accept his proposal. Foolish woman!

He had to focus on the next few weeks, keep his mind on what needed to be done. Then he would confront her and convince her to marry him. That thought caused him to take a deep breath and lift his head as his thoughts considered every move needed to finish up business and board a ship.

RICHARD'S WORDS of comfort to her as they neared the Blackstone estate did little to ease Alaina's mind. During their travel from the Liverpool docks, she'd tried to convince him to return her to Aunt Cornelia's London townhouse. She'd spent the month's voyage building up her courage to face whatever was ahead and she believed that she was as ready as she would ever be. The daily rituals of life on board had helped her to regain a sense of herself. She'd been accepted as just another traveler. As the time passed, the days in Boston that had felt at first like boulders, blocking her ability to see the future, had begun to sift through her mind like sand in an hourglass and dissolve. She would hold her head up and face whatever was before her.

Richard had insisted that they travel immediately to see York and Marielle to find out what had been happening while they were gone. He'd hired a coach and sent a missive off to notify them that they would be arriving in a few days.

As they rode up the long drive that led to the main house, Alaina bit her lip so hard that she drew blood. She almost wished that they were still on the ship where the courage she'd embraced felt genuine.

She feared that if she saw pity or judgment in her friends' eyes, it might be more than she could bear. She couldn't imagine what Marielle had been thinking with regard to her disappearance. And what of Marielle's husband? York radiated power and though he'd always treated her kindly, he was a lord of the realm. Would he have taken part in a pretense to save her reputation? It was unconscionable for them to ask that of him.

She swallowed hard as the coach came to a stop and the door was pulled open. She was left no time to ponder another negative thought. A footman let down the step and offered his hand. As soon as she stepped out of the coach and her foot touched the ground, she lifted her eyes to see Marielle running toward her.

"Thank God, Alaina, you are safe," Marielle blurted out, tears in her eyes as she threw her arms around her. "We were beside ourselves with joy when we received Richard's note that you had arrived. We have prayed day and night for you."

She took a step back, still gripping Alaina's arms. She looked her up and down. "You're thinner and we must remove that look of anxiety from your face and replace it with a smile. Oh Alaina, I can't begin to express my happiness! We must tell York that you are here." She glanced over Alaina's shoulder to Richard. "Oh, forgive me, Richard, I didn't mean to ignore you."

"No apologizes necessary," he said as he turned toward the doorway where Lord Blackstone stood observing the reunion. Giving a nod to Marielle, Richard walked past the women to greet York.

Alaina couldn't speak. She looked from Marielle to York and saw no condemnation, only kindness on their faces. The tears that she'd bottled up inside ran down her face and she no longer tried to stop them from falling as she realized that there was no censure to fear.

Marielle rubbed a gentle finger across Alaina's cheek to wipe away her tears. "Come. I can see I've overwhelmed you. Let's go inside." She folded Alaina's arm in her own and led her toward the entrance. "The hour is late and I can see that you need rest."

When they reached York, he grasped Alaina's hands in his own. "Welcome, my dear." He held her gaze and smiled before loosening his grip and stepping aside so the two women could enter.

Marielle led Alaina into the parlor. Her husband and Richard followed. "York, you must pour us all a glass of sherry to celebrate," Marielle said as she motioned Alaina to sit on the couch.

Alaina took a seat and watched, amazed, as York grinned and saluted his wife. He walked to the liquor cabinet to pour drinks. Richard moved to his side and she could hear the two men talking quietly. Marielle took a seat next to her.

"I...I don't know what to say, Marielle. Your kindness toward me after all this time and what has transpired—"

Marielle held up a hand. "Why, you have spent a lovely time with us in the country," she said, her voice brimming with pleasure. "We have told anyone who asked how much we have appreciated your help over the past few months with our baby Katherine. My cold just lingered on so that I couldn't possibly attend public gatherings, yet you refused to leave until I was well."

Alaina's mouth dropped at Marielle's dramatic outpouring that held a hint of devilish humor.

"No doubt our friends will be happy to see that I am much better," Marielle continued. "Though I would prefer if you would stay on at least for a few more weeks. Now that I am recovering, I should begin to accept invitations and you must attend as well."

Alaina glared at her in awe. "Have you been sick? Your words leave me wondering if you are feverish. You talk as if I never left. I don't know what to say."

Marielle laughed, her eyes sparkling with mischief. "I am feverish with delight that you are here."

York stood before Alaina and offered her a glass of sherry. "I believe my wife and her aunt have found joy in their little scheme. Despite our concern for your safety, we have succeeded in slipping one over on the busybodies who feed on gossip. I personally have enjoyed home life without the pressure of accepting every invitation. My wife's *cold* has encouraged me to stay close to home. So you see, Alaina, we are none the worse and you need only to heal from your journey."

Alaina stared up at York, whose grin reminded her so much of Martin. "You were willing to participate in this pretense? I have no words to express the gratitude I feel in my heart. I am humbled by your generosity." She shook her head slowly from side to side, disbelieving that all her fears and trepidations had been unnecessary. She had refused to believe that her absence could go unnoticed.

"Let us toast." York held up his glass to Richard and to the ladies. "We give thanks for your safe return and to a future less fraught with danger."

They all raised their glasses and Alaina smiled for the first time.

"We look forward to your stay with us," Marielle said, addressing both Alaina and Richard. "I suggest that we catch up tomorrow after a good night's rest." She turned back to Alaina. "Rest assured, your absence has made no waves, other than our anxiety for your safety, but you are here now. We have plenty of time in the days ahead to talk. We expect you to stay with us until you feel ready to leave and share with us only what you feel comfortable. I have sent a letter to Aunt Cornelia to inform her of your arrival. You will find hours of enjoyment when you hear the tales she has told of her visits with you in the country."

"I am speechless," Alaina confessed. She addressed York. "Please know that without your brother's aid, we might—"

"Enough for tonight. Your brother already told me of some of my brother's interventions," York interrupted. "Our little Katherine wakes up quite early in the morning and Marielle refuses to let her nurse be the first one to feed her. It's time for bed. I shall look forward to hearing more about my brother's escapades tomorrow."

"We will appreciate a good night's sleep," Richard said, setting down his glass.

York rang a bell and a servant appeared. Their house servants had been conspicuously out of sight and Alaina realized it was most likely a thoughtful gesture on the part of the Blackstones. She and Richard could avoid surface pleasantries and, perhaps, narrowed eyes.

"Come, Alaina," Richard said, offering a hand.

She stood, paused to give Marielle a hug and York a grateful smile, and followed the servant out.

Chapter Eight

ALAINA SAT in the parlor, her needlework resting in her lap. Weeks had passed since her arrival and the quietness she felt in her spirit could not be measured. Her gratitude was inexpressible, but it was time to resume her life in London.

"Alaina, are you certain that you are ready to return?" York asked as they sat waiting for Marielle and Cornelia to return from the nursery.

"I have imposed on your generosity long enough. I can't begin to tell you how much I appreciate all that you and Marielle have done for me over the past two months. I still find it hard to believe that I will face no repercussions for my disappearance."

"Your time here has been far from an imposition. I must give my wife and Cornelia credit for their inspiration. The ruse was unproblematic. With a newborn, we had no desire to entertain guests. Little Katherine has kept us busy enough."

Alaina smiled, thinking about the precious child. The baby had brightened her stay, especially the dark days she'd spent after her arrival. Once she'd begun to relax, she'd realized that she needed deeper healing. It had less to do with the state of her reputation and more to do with her heart. Her reputation wavered on an edge before she'd left with Harrington and her brother's life held greater value than her standing in society. It was the knowledge that Martin was lost to her that created a far greater impact. An ocean separated them once again, this time without leaving any hope for a dream that needed to be put away permanently.

She had to let him go in her heart. She hoped that her return to London would help ease the gnawing pain that still woke her in the night and ached when York's presence reminded her of his brother.

Marielle and York had been wise enough to leave her be for the first week until Marielle insisted that she take walks with her. Slowly, she began to find enjoyment in her days. She and Richard were closer than ever, though he'd finally returned to his own life after staying on the estate for a couple of weeks.

"I would have appreciated another letter from my wayward brother," York said, taking a sip from the brandy snifter he held. "His last letter spoke of returning with the woman who had accompanied you to America. You have heard nothing more?"

"York, that is not a discussion to have with Alaina," Marielle scolded as she entered the room. "She has enough to think about with leaving for London at the end of the week."

"I didn't mean to pry."

"I don't mind, really." Alaina said as her friend took a seat beside her. Marielle was too intuitive not to know that Alaina had been attracted to Martin before his brother regained the Blackstone estate. She also demonstrated sensitivity toward her when his name was mentioned. There was no way, however, to escape discussions of Martin in

York's presence, but she could guard her thoughts. Obviously Marielle hadn't shared the content of the one letter she'd received, a letter in which Martin had once again offered marriage as a solution to her dishonor.

"I received a letter while you were in Parliament. I should have mentioned it when you returned," Alaina said. "Your brother wrote that Ben, the man who worked for Harrington, asked Molly to marry him soon after the brothel was closed. He'd found another job and a small apartment outside of Boston and nearer to his new position. There is really no reason for Martin to return except to visit you, of course."

"Ah, and here I thought he would be arriving at any time. My business has kept me from hearing the most recent news." He looked over at Marielle, who shrugged.

"I felt it was Alaina's business if she wanted to share the content of her letter."

He gave his wife a look that suggested feigned disappointment that she would keep anything from him. "Regardless, I hope that rapscallion decides to return from America soon. It's time he met his new niece. And where is your aunt? Still with my little princess?"

"Your little princess has been in a mood this evening. Aunt Cornelia is rocking her, hopefully, to sleep for the night."

"Does that mean I'll have some time to spend with my wife?"

Alaina smiled as York stepped closer to Marielle, drew an arm about her and gave her a suggestive leer. Marielle drew her brows together and gave him a disapproving glance, but Alaina didn't miss how her lips curled up slightly. How she envied their love and marital bliss.

An image of Martin intruded in her thoughts. Because of him, she and her brother need never fear Phillip Harrington again. York knew the details of Harrington's demise from Martin's earlier letter to him. She didn't want to know the particulars, only that they were free from his villainy and that Martin hadn't been harmed in the encounter.

At times she wondered what it would have been like if she'd accepted Martin's proposal. Would he have come to love her? But how could he? He'd eventually resent her for boxing him into a loveless marriage when he wanted freedom and adventure.

"I have a surprise for you." Marielle beamed at Alaina. "Now that we can travel more easily with our Kate, we plan to join you in London soon. York has sent a message to our staff to prepare the townhouse. I plan to refurbish my wardrobe and I suspect that you could use some new gowns as well."

"How splendid, Marielle." Alaina reached out and clasped her friend's hands. "You have such a sense of style and I do need new modish gowns."

"We shall take London by storm. I finally have my figure back and I plan on making the most of it," Marielle said, grinning at her husband.

"Enough of that." York frowned. "I happen to have enjoyed your plumpness before and after

Katherine's birth. I shall not appreciate my wife being gawked at again. You caused me countless concerns in the past. Married or not, too many rakes still attempt to garner your attention."

"Not with you standing over me every minute, guarding your property."

Alaina laughed at her two friends as they poked jibes at one another. She was relieved to know that Marielle would join her in London for a time. She didn't want them to know that fear still crept in at the thought of facing London society again.

She gathered her knitting and rose from her seat. "I believe I'll retire early tonight."

York stood and nodded. "We wish you a peaceful night's sleep, Alaina." He looked at his wife. "What do you say, my dear? I'm feeling a bit tired myself." He winked at Marielle who returned a half-smirking grin before hugging Alaina and bidding her goodnight.

Alaina went upstairs, stopping for only a moment at the open nursery door. Aunt Cornelia must have gone to bed. She tiptoed in and gazed at the sleeping baby, knowing how much she would miss the child and wondering if she would ever have a family of her own.

MARTIN CURSED at the storm that delayed the ship's crossing. It had taken him longer than expected to finish his business in Virginia and in Boston before he could board a ship home. He'd hoped they'd reach England by week's end but the storm made it impossible to gain any distance. They were most likely going to lose another few days, he thought dismally.

He was haunted by his thoughts of Alaina's fate upon her return to London. The ton enjoyed chewing on every tidbit of gossip. They'd feasted for months on the news of her father's disgrace and untimely death. Now they were most likely feeding on her scandalous behavior. She would be more of a recluse than she'd been during her mourning year. He hadn't received any news from England but he wasn't surprised. With his constant travel, he could have missed a letter, even if one had been sent. His days had been busy and his nights filled with anxiety. He wanted Alaina with him, safe from society's scourge and in his arms.

Foolish woman, to leave with that scoundrel, regardless of the reason, he thought as he looked out at the rough sea. She was the willing martyr for those she loved. Blast it! Martin brushed back his windblown hair. *And where was I? She might have come to me if I'd been there.*

Ben, who had convinced Molly to stay in America and marry him, told Martin of Harrington's fate. The two men who showed up at the brothel, and using an interpreter, talked to Ben who'd remained guarding the place. He confirmed that the businessman, who they called Harrington, was Mr. Cox to the workers at the gambling hall and brothel.

Before Harrington could disentangle himself and escape the brothel, the two men had confronted him. From what Ben had said, it had been a bloody scene. They had beaten him up and left him unconscious. Ben took on the responsibility of calling the authorities. By the time they'd arrived he'd succumbed to his injuries.

No great loss, as far as Martin was concerned. No one else would become his victim. Martin was pleased with the outcome. He thought about his last observation of the slimy perpetrator, squirming on the floor begging for mercy. After what he'd done to Alaina, the consequences were fitting and just.

As he watched the heaving mounds of water crash against the side of the ship, his worry over Alaina's disgrace returned. There was no way that she or Richard could explain her journey to America without leaving questions in everyone's mind. Martin refused to dwell on the weeks that she'd spent with Harrington. It was in the past and she'd truly believed she was saving her brother from prison. He hoped that she was healing from the trauma of what may have occurred. *But what must she be experiencing now that she's returned?*

If she'd agreed to stay in America, they would be married by now. He'd had such little time to talk with her and when he had, he'd done a poor job of apologizing and a worse job of proposing. He needed to see her and convince her that they were meant to be together.

Perhaps, now that she's faced society's censure, she has realized that her refusal was foolish. The vultures of the ton would not dare to shun her as his wife. He gripped the side rails and bathed his face in the icy spray of the waves and considered their future.

The wilderness drew him but at the same time

he felt the loneliness that accompanies a stranger in a new land. If Alaina would only agree to be his wife, they could both put the past behind them and start anew. In Virginia, she would be forever free of scandal and free to be herself in the new world.

Wiping his face with the sleeve of his damp coat, he trod carefully along the water-soaked boards of the ship, staying out of the way of the crew while planning with each step. If she accepted his proposal but refused to live in America, then he'd sell his land. No matter how much he loved his new life in the wilderness of Virginia, her needs must come first.

If she says no and sends me away... He sucked in a labored breath at the dismal thought that clouded his plans and left him with a feeling of emptiness as he retreated to his cabin.

THE SHIP anchored in the dead of night in the pounding rain. It was bad enough that the voyage took ten days longer than it should have, but Martin's trip to the Blackstone estate from Liverpool seemed endless. He needed to see his brother and freshen up before leaving for London.

Upon his arrival, George, the Blackstones' butler, opened the door cautiously and nearly fell back on his heels when he saw Martin standing there. Grinning from ear to ear, he ushered him in and asked if he should wake York. "He has been worried about you, Master Martin, and Milady, as well. You look exhausted." George's eyes dropped to Martin's drenched clothing. "Wet, as well. Perhaps you might want to warm yourself by the fire and gain a good night's rest first?"

"Good idea, George. The morning is soon enough to see my brother. If you'll have one of the servants bring my baggage to my bedchamber, I'm going to the kitchen. I am famished."

"Forgive me. I should have thought to offer you something to eat. The cook has retired but I'll gladly prepare a meal."

"Nonsense, I am quite accustomed to taking care of myself. I'll have no problem finding something to tide me over until morning."

The butler gave a thankful nod. "I'll see to your room and baggage."

Martin left for the kitchen, feeling the comforting warmth of hearth and home.

MARTIN HAD barely opened his eyes the next morning when he heard an infant's cry. By the time his eyes adjusted to his surroundings, the cries had stopped and he heard giggles as the sounds faded in the distance.

Realizing the babe must have woken to be fed, he rose to wash and dress. He still couldn't picture his older brother as a father and looked forward to seeing the transformation and meet the child. His stay would be brief. He wanted to talk to Marielle and get some information before going to see Alaina. As Alaina's closest friend, she'd know how she was coping with society's rebuffs.

When he entered the breakfast parlor, he found York alone, sipping coffee and smiling at him as if he had never left.

"Welcome, little brother. I nearly fell out of bed

this morning when I heard you had arrived. By the looks of you, I'd say you could use more than a cup of coffee. Did you sleep in those clothes?"

Martin smiled indulgently. "Slept, ate and became rain-soaked in them, I'm afraid."

York laughed as he stood to give his brother a hug and a slap on the back. "By god, we wondered if you'd ever return. We thought the new world might have swallowed you up."

Martin poured himself a cup of coffee and helped himself to bread and cheese from the sideboard before joining his brother at the table.

"After finishing up with the Harrington business, I had to settle my own business before finding passage on a ship. I hope you received the letter I wrote."

"Yes. I wrote back without getting a reply."

"Never received it. I had to spend a good deal of time in Virginia and then back again to Boston."

"I understand. Your adventure with that villain, Harrington, must have felt like old times."

"Very much like it. I had no problem remembering the skills we learned on the streets. Once the scoundrel was adequately taken care of I needed to settle my affairs. I'd bought horses and supplies that needed to be transported to Virginia. I've purchased some beauties, York." He paused to sip his coffee. "I needed to meet with my overseer, set up a work schedule and hire some ranch hands. I accomplished a great deal in a short time, though it took longer than I'd hoped to book passage back."

"I'm glad you're home, but why such sudden

haste?"

Martin took a bite of cheese. He didn't want to tell his brother that he planned to persuade Alaina to marry him. She might refuse him again and he didn't want his brother's questions or his commiseration. "I was concerned about the Craymores. Is Richard well? How is Alaina fairing?"

"Richard is doing fine. Best to ask my wife about Alaina." York's eyes turned toward the open doorway.

Marielle swept into the room with the baby in her arms. Her faithful dog, Beatrice, followed close behind, her ears perking up at the sight of Martin.

"It is you and as devilishly handsome. Though I must say those clothes and that beard..."

Martin rose from his seat. "I fell into bed last night and was dead asleep in less than a minute. This morning I was too restless to see you to take time to shave. Never mind my appearance, a welcome is in order." He enveloped her and the little package in her arms. Loosening his hold, he stared at the baby who was wriggling about.

"And who is this little creature? I expected a tiny babe, Marielle, not a squirming chit. What are you feeding the child?"

"Meet your niece, Katherine Anna, named after your mother. Kate, meet your errant uncle. You have been gone far too long. Perhaps you forget when she was born," Marielle scolded. "She is approaching six months without having laid eyes on her uncle in all that time."

Martin ruffled the baby's golden curls and

grinned sheepishly. "You have honored my mother, but I suppose I shall need to win this little one's favor."

Katherine lifted her head out of the crook of her mother's arms, her big blue eyes gazing up at Martin before she spied her father. She stretched out her chubby arms to York and squealed.

Martin grinned as York reached out and took the child from her mother's arms. Placing her comfortably on his lap, he gave her a kiss and a squeeze. The baby giggled and gave him a wet kiss on his nose.

"Brother, you have become domesticated," Martin chuckled. "Marielle, what have you done to him?"

"I beg your pardon," she chided as she took her seat. "Your brother had as much to do with it. If you could see him rolling about the floor with Kate, you would think he was barely out of the schoolroom himself."

"If our old cronies on the street could see you now," Martin joked as he petted Beatrice who was wagging her tail and nudging his pant leg with her nose.

"Braum already has," York said, pushing his coffee cup out of the baby's grasp.

"Braum is still about? He's managed to keep himself out of jail?"

"Not only that, he has even settled down with that pretty barmaid he enjoyed frolicking with at Shipley's Tavern. It seems she is about to deliver and make Braum a proud papa."

When Marielle rose to take the baby from York,

Martin realized they had left her out of their recollections.

"Marielle, you are as beautiful as ever."

"Watch it now, Martin. You will cause my wife to become vain."

"I speak the truth."

"And you haven't lost your ability for sweet talk," Marielle said with a wink. "I want to hear all about your time in America, but first I must tell you why I am even more excited that you are here." She clapped the baby's hands in her own. "Alaina and my aunt are here. They are most likely still sleeping. This little one refuses to let me sleep the morning away. No doubt they will be pleased that you have arrived."

Martin nearly choked on the chunk of bread he'd been chewing.

Marielle continued, appearing not to notice his reaction. "We have waited to baptize Katherine in the hopes that you would return. You will agree to be her godfather?"

"I'd be honored," he mumbled, still trying to take in the news that Alaina was upstairs. He'd be able to talk to her before night's end. He tightened his jaw, his eyes lowered to the plate set before him, though he saw nothing. Declarations raced through his mind and determination caused him to grind his teeth in anticipation. By midnight tonight he would convince Alaina that she was his and that they belonged together.

"I'd like to hear more excitement in your voice, Martin. Martin?"

Marielle's voice seemed far away as he shook

himself out of his trance and looked at his sister-in-law, who wore an expectant expression. "Forgive me, your news of Alaina's visit caught me off guard. There is nothing I would like better than to be Katherine's godfather." He watched as Marielle shot an amused glance at her husband.

"Alaina is to be the godmother, so you see, your timing is perfect."

Martin nodded. She was right. The time of his arrival appeared to be ideal. A few moments passed in awkward silence before he reined in his thoughts. "How is Alaina coping? I can only imagine what she faced when she returned to London."

"Erase that grim expression, Martin," Marielle said, reaching her hand over to his. "She is doing remarkably well. Aunt Cornelia managed to do a superb job keeping the *haute ton* appraised of Alaina's welfare during the time of her *stay* with us."

"She stayed with you after her arrival?"

"York, you didn't tell him of our ruse?"

"I haven't had the chance. I'm sure you'll relish telling him yourself."

Marielle pushed her chair closer to Martin, settling the baby comfortably in her lap. "I certainly will." She wore a Cheshire cat grin as she filled him in with the details. When she finished, she sat back, kissing the top of Kate's head. "Why, even the most austere society matrons had not an *inkling* that Alaina was out of England."

Martin gaped at her. "I'm stunned. All along I thought that she was suffering all manner of disgrace," he murmured, more to himself than anyone else. His mind struggled with the disparity of what he'd assumed was Alaina's fate and the actuality of her reception.

Marielle rested her chin on the baby's head and continued. "Aunt Cornelia truly enjoyed the farce. You do know how she loves to tell tales. When we heard the news of Alaina's disappearance, we feared for her safety and there was nothing we could do to help her, except to protect her reputation. While York and I maintained that she was here helping with our Kate, my aunt continued on with her usual social calendar. When she was asked about Alaina, she told them she'd left London to stay with us for the summer. When anyone questioned her extended visit, she went on about the bad cold I was struggling with and Alaina's kindness for helping with the baby. Since she'd been in seclusion most of year anyway, her absence from social affairs was easily accepted."

Marielle's eyes sparkled as she talked of Aunt Cornelia's capers. "She had to spend hours educating Alaina on her tales just in case one of them came up in conversation. I believe one story had to do with Alaina falling off a horse into a bramble bush and limping back to the estate with dozens of thorns stuck to her gown."

Martin's lips curled at the image. "Cornelia has never lost her sense of humor. How old is she now?" he asked, trying to force his mind from thoughts that could not be shared. He'd expected to save her from ruin and it appeared she didn't need him.

"That is a question you mustn't ask her," Marielle teased. "'We shan't talk about that' is her standard reply. She is as lively as ever and I imagine that she will jump for joy when she sees you. She asks about you often and has wondered, as we have, why there was so little news from you. Martin, more letters would have put us at ease," she scolded.

"We must be thankful he is home safe, my dear," York interrupted.

"Most definitely, but do not be surprised, Martin, if my aunt doesn't admonish you as well."

"And I will accept it with great humility." He bowed his head in mock shame only to snap his head up when Katherine let out a scream of pleasure, causing everyone to turn their attention to her antics.

"We will need to find you a suitable wardrobe until yours are cleaned and pressed," York said, tossing aside his napkin. "Meanwhile, I'd like to show you the renovations that have been completed. When we return, Alaina and Cornelia should be up and about."

"Perhaps I should tell him a bit more about Alaina's stay—"

"Marielle," York interrupted. "Shouldn't Katherine be having her bath now? In fact, Martin could use one too, but we'll venture out first. I suspect that Martin's old horse, Jupiter, will be neighing and prancing about in his stall as soon as he smells his presence."

Acknowledging her husband's obvious signal for her to say no more, Marielle wrapped the baby in her arms and rose from her chair.

Martin stood, puzzled at the look that passed between his brother and Marielle. He reached out to hold Katherine's tiny hand. The baby grasped his finger.

"What a grip the child has. She'll be holding the reins of a pony in no time. Yes, a pony may be my first gift to her," Martin said, realizing that the child had already captured his heart.

"If your brother doesn't beat you to it. The minute she sat up on her own, he was ready to buy her one."

The baby seemed to know that she was the subject of conversation as she babbled with glee. Martin laughed and kissed her chubby fingers. "I plan to tell her of all the mischief her father's been involved in so that she will not idolize him so."

"She'll not believe a word of it," York countered. "Now let's see what we can do about your shabby appearance."

YORK AND Martin spent a good part of the morning catching up on each other's news while riding about the estate. When they returned, George had miraculously appeared with a set of clothing, aired and freshly pressed, that Martin had left behind before leaving for America. After washing and dressing, Martin looked once again like a stately, clean-shaven English gentleman. Only his boots belied his travels. George did his best to fill in the cuts and scratches, buffing the dark-brown leather to a mirrored sheen. His worn boots were the least of Martin's concerns.

"I'd like to hear more about Alaina's progress," he said, taking a seat in front of York's desk. "I am surprised that I haven't seen her or Cornelia yet."

"They were here briefly while you were in your bedchamber. I suspect that they are in the nursery with Marielle. She has told them of your arrival. They'll be down presently for luncheon," he paused to look at his watch, "which should be very soon. I know that you have been worried about Alaina. Not to worry, brother. She is doing marvelously well. Actually, she is planning to leave for London in a few days."

"I am thankful that you, Marielle and Cornelia were able to protect her from disgrace." As he spoke, the thought that she had no need of his proposal deflated his previous fervor to offer for her hand the moment he saw her. Would she refuse him again?

"We had one matter that needed to be dealt with once the ruse was set in motion," York said. "We had to convince Priscilla that her silence was to her benefit. As it turned out, she was as much a victim of Harrington's scams as Alaina. When we confronted her, the woman pleaded for forgiveness."

Martin nearly missed York's news about the widow. He was still absorbing that Alaina was doing "marvelously well". Richard had told him of Priscilla Dunfly's intrusion into Alaina's life and the woman's conspiracy with Harrington. He could hardly see her as a victim. "She doesn't deserve forgiveness."

"That's how we felt until we heard her story,"

York said. "We found out that she was in dire straits. Her late husband was heavy in debt, leaving her penniless when he died and with an elderly mother who needed constant care. Creditors were demanding payment. Worse, they expected that she would erase the debts by allowing them into her bedroom. When Harrington offered to free her of debt by helping him complete a business transaction, she listened. He presented himself as a charming and earnest gentleman who needed Alaina's cooperation. Her cooperation would grant him what he needed and Priscilla's desperate situation would be resolved. He pledged that Alaina would come to no harm. Once Priscilla befriended her and met Richard, she didn't want to go through with it, but Harrington threatened her and used the same evidence against Richard to convince her to cooperate. You know the rest of the story."

"You're saying that she felt that Alaina's reputation held less value than Richard's life." Martin frowned, rubbing his chin. He still felt disgust at the widow's behavior.

"Exactly right," York agreed. "She felt cornered by her own desperation and Harrington's evidence against Richard. Knowing Alaina's devotion to her brother, she saw no other way, except to help her go to America and complete the business. Thanks to you, Martin, Alaina returned safely and Richard is doing well. There appeared to be no reason to shame the woman more. I suggested that she leave London to avoid any additional problems. I found a cottage in Yorkshire for her and her mother and I dealt with the creditors."

Martin doubted he could have been as generous to such a woman. "She betrayed Alaina with her false friendship."

"And Alaina forgave her. Desperation can lead us to do things against our character. Alaina believed Priscilla was making the right decision. Though she made no excuses, she was forthright in her explanations of the entire situation. We expected that Richard would ostracize her, but Alaina reminded him of their family history. Priscilla's humility and repentance charmed him. We even suspect that a romance might be brewing.

"But enough of that. No doubt everything would have turned out differently, Martin, if you had not interceded. Alaina will be happy to see that you have returned safely as well. She has gone through a great deal, as you well know. She returned not only dispirited but ashamed. We have done our best to encourage her to put the past behind her. She may be reluctant to face you. After all, you were witness to her...time with Harrington."

"I hold nothing against her. She believed she was helping Richard."

"Regardless, she dealt with a great deal of self-incrimination though she has shown the strong spirit that we knew she's been endowed with. She is also a survivor and you will see that these qualities have been revived in her. I confess that Marielle fears that your arrival may rekindle those feelings. Be patient with her."

"Patient?" Martin grimaced. "She may not have

told you that I offered her marriage before she left Boston. I wanted to protect from what I expected she would face on her return. I thought I'd find her in the depths of despair."

"And you wanted to save her again?"

Martin winced at his brother's words.

York smiled. "Stop trying to be her savior."

Martin glared at his brother. The wisdom of his words caused him to twist in his seat. He wanted to be more than her savior. He prided himself on being able to make fair assessments and stand his ground but the ground beneath him felt suddenly unsteady. He thought he'd been prepared with solid reasoning that would convince Alaina to accept his proposal. Now he had no idea how to proceed.

Chapter Nine

ALAINA SPLASHED water on her face and dried it with a towel. Glancing in her mirror, she tucked a curl behind her ear. Though the blue day dress she wore was simple, it would suffice, and she was glad that her hair was pinned neatly back with a ribbon. She'd had no need to fuss with her appearance in the company of her friends, but Martin was here. She remembered all too well the wrinkled gown and her unkempt hair at their last meeting in a Boston hotel.

When Marielle had told her and Aunt Cornelia of Martin's return, Alaina had done her best to mask the emotions that had surged through her. Cornelia had been ecstatic and had wanted to rush down to see him while Alaina's first reaction had been to rush to her bedchamber to absorb the news.

Alaina had been grateful when Marielle had urged them to wait until luncheon, allowing York to spend more time with his brother. Alaina suspected that Marielle understood her need to prepare herself to see Martin again.

She wondered how she would manage to make it through the next few days with him so close. Her rejection of his proposal would certainly hang in the air between them, and the feelings she'd so carefully packed away were suddenly in the forefront of her thoughts.

It seemed her life would never go according to

a well-appointed plan. She hadn't expected to see him again, though surely he would have returned to visit his brother and his family eventually.

But today?

Perhaps it was a blessing that she had little time to prepare for his visit. She might have ordered a coach immediately to escape seeing him.

Taking one last look in her mirror, she decided that she'd successfully pulled herself together and was ready to face Martin. She rose from her seat just as someone rapped on the bedroom door.

"Yes?"

"Alaina, are you ready to go downstairs?" Marielle asked through the closed door.

Alaina took a deep breath and opened the door to find Marielle smiling and holding Katherine.

Her friend's grin faded. "You look pale. If you need more time—"

"I'm fine," she lied, though she had little doubt Marielle knew it and understood. "Where is Aunt Cornelia?"

"I couldn't restrain her from seeing Martin and it's all for the best. No doubt she has already relayed the stories she created of the ruse. I felt you needed time alone."

Alaina nodded, she appreciated her friend's sensitivity. She straightened her shoulders, brushed down her skirt, and as she followed Marielle down the staircase, she pinched her cheeks. As they walked toward the dining room, she lifted her chin and prepared to wear a smile when she confronted Martin.

As they approached the room, she slowed her

steps, causing Marielle to pause and grasp her arm.

"Alaina, are you sure you're all right?"

"Of course, I look forward to seeing Martin." She forced a cheery smile. "I owe him much gratitude."

Marielle gave a tilt of her head, as if questioning her friend's countenance.

The two men stood as soon as the two women walked in. Aunt Cornelia remained seated.

"Well, they have finally arrived," York said, taking the few steps to Marielle and taking the baby from her.

"Alaina," Martin said softly as his eyes caught hers.

"Martin," she murmured, ignoring her heart that refused to remain still.

The room grew silent as they two stood, staring at each other. Aunt Cornelia broke the silence. "Alaina, who would have thought that the day would bring Martin to the door? We have had such a delightful talk. He tells me that his voyage took much longer than he expected, but he is here safe and sound. No doubt the two of you have much to catch up on, and I have taken up too much of his time. I do tend to go on and on."

Alaina relaxed her body, which had grown rigid and gave Cornelia a grateful smile. Leave it to her to ease the tension of the moment.

"Cook has put on a larger spread than usual for Martin's benefit. Let us sit and enjoy her labor. I believe my brother has had few decent meals since he left America."

Everyone took a seat and York set Kate on his

lap and began to tickle her. She giggled in return.

"Please don't get her all riled up," Marielle said. "I am hoping she'll take a long nap this afternoon. She has been a bundle of energy this morning."

The baby reached up and rubbed her father's cheek. York grinned and kissed her chubby fingers. "Have you been wearing your mother out, love?" As he snuggled Katherine in his arms, footmen walked in holding silver trays.

Matty, the baby's nurse, tapped on the open door. Waiting for her mistress's nod, she walked in and stretched her arms out to collect her charge.

"You are taking my princess away so soon?" York asked, tickling Katherine under her chin.

"She's ready for sleep, my lord. Your little one has gone through two outfits this morning and it appears that she has drooled on this one as well," Matty said, smiling at him as she lifted the child into her arms and walked toward the door.

"I have just begun to realize the expense of having two women in the house," York said with a groan. "I can only imagine the future clothing bills."

"You'll spoil both of them rotten," Martin said, offering his first grin since Alaina had arrived.

"No doubt," York said, with a more than tolerant twist of his lips. He raised his glass, having already asked a footman to pour everyone some of his finest wine. "Here is to the remarkable arrival of my brother from the land of mystery and adventure."

Alaina, who could no longer focus on the baby,

lifted her glass to see Martin staring at her. She gave him a hint of a smile, took a sip, and set her glass down.

"I have heard little about your land in Virginia, Martin. Please tell us more," Marielle said, directing the conversation.

Martin acknowledged her question. He glanced at Alaina as he described his purchase as if he wanted her approval. York and Marielle continued to ask him more questions as a footman walked around the table, pouring soup into bowls.

Much to Alaina's relief, the hour passed quickly. She suspected that no one wanted to bring up painful memories and although she wanted to thank Martin for his intervention in America, she feared it would cause the discussion to turn dismal. She could see by the look on York's face that he was happy to have his brother at his table.

She sipped her soup and nibbled on some fruit and cheese, doing her best to appear pleased by Martin's presence and the conversation. Thankfully, no one pressured her to answer questions or join in the conversation.

When York tossed his napkin on the table, Martin patted his lips with his own and set it down. "Alaina, would you care to walk with me through the gardens?"

Surprised at his sudden request, she looked to her host and hostess and was certain she saw them both breathe sighs of relief.

"The afternoon is only a little cool. We'll sit on the veranda and observe while you two enjoy the garden paths," Marielle said, looking at York and her aunt for acceptance.

"I have some work to finish in my study. Go enjoy," York said, rising from his seat.

Alaina stood and walked with Martin out to the veranda, her nerves on edge. Marielle and Cornelia followed them out the balcony doors and took a seat, waving them off.

Martin led her down the steps and onto the brick path. They strolled in silence until they reached a pond edged with water lilies. Alaina knelt and smoothed her fingers over one of the rubbery petals. "Water lilies hold such beauty," she murmured, thankful that her voice sounded calm and even, rather than reflecting her trepidation. "They simply grow to please the eye, free to blossom with little care."

"On the contrary," Martin said as he knelt beside her. "They have a very special purpose in life, to keep the pond water healthy and clear. They provide shelter and safety for fish by blocking sunlight and shielding them from predators. They are not only helpful but self-sacrificing flowers. Much like you."

Alaina snapped her head toward him and met his gaze.

"Since we've met, Alaina, you have been bent on trying to save others from harm at a great cost to yourself. Your brother told me how you tried to protect your mother from your father's brutal hand, bringing his wrath upon you. Your desire to shield your brother from harm was commendable, though dangerous and even foolhardy. I hope your experience has taught you that."

Alaina stiffened, feeling like a child being disciplined. "I am not certain of your intended meaning, Martin, but I assure you I do not plan any more hazardous adventures."

The lilies forgotten, she stood and straightened her skirt. Spying a nearby bench, she walked over to it, sat and clasped her hands tightly on her lap. Martin approached and joined her too close for her comfort.

"I have been fortunate enough not to suffer the consequences of my actions, Martin. I understand that you have been concerned. You can put your mind to rest. I am doing well," she said, staring straight ahead to avoid his probing gaze.

"I'm thankful that your experience can be put behind you."

She turned back and saw in his expression that he meant what he said. "I haven't had the opportunity to truly thank you for rescuing me. You put yourself at great risk. Something could have gone wrong." Her voice softened. "I never would have forgiven myself if you had been injured, or worse."

Martin raised a staying hand. "Alaina—"

"Please, let me finish. I do not want to think of what you may have saved me from." Her voice faltered.

"You don't need to thank me."

"But I do." She could feel the heat of his stare. She felt flustered and uncomfortably warm. She inched away from him.

"Alaina, Harrington weaseled his way into people's lives and used them to his advantage. He sensed your devotion to your brother. You did what you thought was best. I understand that the widow that helped you leave was also taken in by him, though she betrayed your trust."

"Priscilla. She didn't coerce me. I made the decision. Yes, I felt betrayed but Harrington caught her in a web of deceit as well. Regardless, I hope I have become more cautious and will be more discerning when making acquaintances. And how have you spent the past few months?" she asked, trying to take the attention away from her past actions. "I appreciated the letter I received telling me of what occurred when you confronted...him." She couldn't bring herself to say Harrington's name. She'd tried to erase it from her memory. "I understand that Molly chose to stay in America."

"Yes, the girl appeared quite content with Ben and under his protection she had no desire to return to London. I would have left America sooner but I had affairs to settle in Virginia. As I mentioned in our discussion at the table, I purchased hundreds of acres. I'm not certain what will come of it but the idea of breeding horses and cattle appeals to me. The land is magnificent, Alaina. If you could see it, I think you'd be in awe of its beauty."

She saw his eyes brighten as he spoke of his land. That was where his heart lies, she thought, and hers felt as heavy as crushed stone.

"I had supplies and livestock that I needed to transport safely. Coach travel was my only recourse and the roads are poor. It took far longer than I would have hoped. After taking care of affairs there, I returned to Boston on horseback in record time but still it took a few weeks."

She listened as he appeared tense, speaking faster than usual. What was he trying to tell her?

"A few days were lost on the way to Virginia because of a problem wheel and of course, the horses needed rest." He took a breath and twisted his upper body toward hers. "Alaina, I didn't want you to leave." He reached out and pushed a curl away from her cheek. "I feared for you. You had already faced enough scandal."

She felt the warmth of his touch and shook off the impulse to reach out to him. "Yes, I know. You offered to marry me to save me from ruin. You must realize now that it was unnecessary." She focused on the whiteness of the lilies, caught their slight movement as a toad hopped onto one and disappeared beneath its wide leaves.

"As you have already heard, I did not have to face public censure. I shall be forever grateful to Aunt Cornelia, Marielle and York. I doubt I shall ever forget my horrid experiences in America or your heroic actions but my friends have helped me to heal." She wanted to make it clear that she did not need any more sacrifices from him. He could return to America free to live as he chose.

"I fear you may have hurried back to England out of concern for my well-being," she continued, not allowing him to interrupt. "If that is true, I apologize for not writing and telling you that my reputation was well protected. In truth, I did not deserve to escape ridicule. I caused much worry to all who cared about me and you well know of my scandalous behavior. Regardless, I have found healing and contentment here and have succeeded in making peace with my past. I believe I am ready to return to my life in London."

"You deserve peace and security, nothing less." Martin reached out, clasped her arms, and drew her to him. Before she could draw back, he lowered his lips to hers, barely touching them, brushing them softly with his own. "I have missed you, Alaina," he whispered hoarsely.

Alaina felt his warm breath mingle with hers. She said nothing, not knowing how to respond. Nothing had prepared her for this. She knew she should pull away, protect herself from the onslaught of emotions she'd worked so hard to contain.

But her body resisted her thoughts.

He drew her closer. An uncontrolled sigh escaped her lips and the passion she'd thought was lost to her seeped through her defenses.

His lips met hers, caressed them and became more demanding. He drew her into a more intimate embrace. His warm breath waking feelings of need inside her as his lips began to leave small kisses along her cheekbone to the hollow of her neck.

His boldness woke her from her trance. She pushed him away while attempting to clear her head. How could she so easily forget the promises she'd made to herself?

He dropped his arms to her sides, gazed into her eyes, his own smoldering with desire.

"Martin, what is it you want from me?" she

breathed, trying to still her pounding heart.

"You say you are content, but I see more in your eyes, Alaina. I see desire unquenched. I want to hold you, kiss you. I want to make you mine." He tried to pull her close again.

She brushed his arms away. "You've kissed me before and *left*. You desire to be free and make your home in America. I can feel that in you, hear it in your words. I have my own desires, to create a life for myself *here*."

Alaina looked down, picked at a strand of thread that had pulled free from an embroidered flower on her gown. "Martin, I am tired of conflicts and confusion," she said, her voice almost sorrowful. "I want..."

"I want you, Alaina."

Alaina stopped tugging at the thread, stood, smoothed her skirt and glared down at him. "You want me." She paused and looked into his eyes, her heart suddenly calm. "Is that all?" she asked in barely a whisper.

"What do you mean is that all?" He pushed himself from the seat and walked toward the pond. Picking up a stone, he skipped it across the water.

She stared at his back, surprised at his sudden anger. "Martin, I don't believe you know what you want." She waited for him to say more, needed him to, but he remained silent, staring out over the pond before turning around slowly.

"I had hoped that you would reconsider my proposal, Alaina. I have feared for you and the pain society could have caused you. I wanted—"

"Is that why you returned?" She shook her

head in sudden understanding. "Fortunately, your altruism is not needed," she said. "I believe I have made that clear." She turned and strutted away but slowed and looked back to see him standing stock still, a puzzled look on his face.

"At least your visit is not wasted, Martin." Her lips turned up into an almost wistful smile. "You have met your niece and we are to be her godparents. Your return has not been in vain." She broadened her smile and walked on ahead. When she reached the veranda, she found Marielle and Cornelia chatting cheerfully together, obviously unaware of Martin's overtures and her brief surrender. They looked first at her and then behind her. "Where's Martin?" Marielle asked.

"The day has grown cooler and I didn't bring a wrap. He's..." She turned when she heard his footfalls on the steps. "Do you mind, Marielle, if I go to the nursery to see Katherine? I won't wake her."

"Of course not." Marielle gave her a questioning look. "Would you like me to go with you?"

"No, I need some time alone," she admitted, knowing that she'd used a visit to the nursery as an excuse. She could hear Martin approaching them. "I...I'm sorry." Before either woman could say another word, she fled through the balcony doors and up to her room. She closed the door behind her. Leaning against it, she let out a ragged sigh. She'd been abrupt with Marielle, rude, in fact, and to Aunt Cornelia as well. She was behaving wretchedly. She walked over to the bed and sat on the edge. She would need to make her apologies. *Thank goodness we're leaving soon. How will I get through the next few days?*

"The man turns my heart inside out," she muttered to herself before covering her face with her hands, her mind relieving her time alone with Martin.

I've been doing so well. For the first time in a long time, I have been able to consider what I wanted — or thought I wanted. Drat! He creates chaos in my mind. What does he mean, he wants me? No mention of love, not for me, but when he talks of his dreams, his land, his eyes light up.

She untied the ribbon that held her hair in place and tossed it aside. Martin would be miserable living a normal, everyday life. He needed adventure, she knew. She could even understand it. He'd spent too many of his formative years living on the streets when he should have been living as the son of an aristocrat. She curled up on the bed and drew her arms around her as her eyes filled with tears. *But will I ever be able to forget him?*

Her confusing thoughts were interrupted by a knock on the door. She sat up and tried to shake off her lapse into weakness.

Cornelia opened the door slightly and peeked in. "I am sorry to disturb you, my dear. I can come back later."

She brushed away the unwanted tears. "Please, come in."

She rose from the bed and walked over and looked at herself in the bedroom mirror. Her hair was a sight and her cheeks red.

"I thought perhaps I might be of help to you,"

Cornelia said, treading lightly with her words.

"Would I be rude to ask for dinner in my room tonight?" Alaina asked, eyeing Cornelia through the mirror. "I'm really not feeling up to facing everyone."

Cornelia tilted her head to the side and observed Alaina. "Do you really want to spend the night in your room? I have no idea what you and Martin discussed, but he too took off after your walk together. Perhaps your misunderstanding could be resolved. I believe the two of you care very much for each other."

"There is no misunderstanding. We both want different things."

"You deserve to have your heart's desire. I only ask that you think deeply about what that is."

"Oh, why does everything have to be so difficult?" Alaina groaned, sweeping her arms out in frustration. "Why must there always be a price to pay? I've found some peace over the past couple of months. You must see that. I will always be grateful to Martin and I am glad he has returned safely. I see the joy on York's and Marielle's faces to have him here, but I admit his presence causes me to step back into my uncertainty and confusion."

Cornelia stood silently, wearing an almost pleased expression after Alaina's outburst. She breathed a sigh of frustration, sat down at her vanity table and started pulling out her hairpins. She and Cornelia had lived together long enough for the woman to know her almost better than she knew herself.

Cornelia walked over and, waving Alaina's

hand away, pulled out the remaining pins and, picking up a hairbrush, began to brush Alaina's hair. When she set down the brush, she drew up Alaina's long curls, pulling them smoothly into a twist and pinning it into place without saying a word.

She chose a jeweled hair comb lying on the vanity and nestled it securely into the side of the chignon. "Lovely." Stepping back, she admired her handiwork. "Now, young lady, it is time that you dressed for dinner."

MARTIN MARCHED out the front door after Alaina escaped the veranda. He was too agitated to attempt any social contact. He walked to the stables and to Jupiter's stall. Jupiter was getting on in years but they had shared a past together. He had found it difficult to leave the horse behind when he left for America. Jupiter whinnied at the sight of him and nudged Martin's face. Martin returned the greeting by patting his mane.

"You want to go for another ride, old boy?" He opened the stall and led his horse out of the stable. Jupiter was accustomed to Martin riding him bareback with only a bridle. He stood in place while Martin secured the bridle and mounted him. He eased the horse toward a well-ridden path.

Once the stable was out of sight, he led him into a gallop. As he rode, he went over his conversation with Alaina. *I told her I wanted her, damn it. What does she expect from me? I need her to tell me if she has no feelings for me.* He thought of how she had sighed in his arms. *Damn, I must make her see that she is making a mistake.*

Martin nudged the horse toward a nearby stream and let him drink. His mind returned to their unexpected meeting in America and to her time with Harrington.

He hadn't wanted to think about it, but she had lived with the man. She was most likely no longer an innocent. Her entrance to society again might not be as smooth as she hoped. It didn't matter to Martin if she had lost her virginity. He had been in enough trouble in his past not to demand purity, but another suitor might expect it.

Alaina was a victim. He could only imagine what the weeks spent with Harrington must have been like for her. He wanted to make up for it. He was ready to marry her, start a family, save her from any disgrace that might arise if news of her time with Harrington ever became public. Despite the ruse, there was always that possibility.

He rode on, allowing his thoughts to wander while his frustration grew. What was he doing? He was trying to find reasons to convince Alaina to marry him. Why was he delving into a past he knew she needed to forget? How else could he convince her?

Bringing the horse to a halt on the top of a hill, he looked out at the distant mountains. The setting sun created a blur of pinks and lavenders. As it descended, the sky darkened, the colors became more vibrant and suddenly he knew why she had rejected him.

She wanted, needed security and dependability. He couldn't blame her. She had never felt safe, even as a child. He had been afraid of commitment, of settling down to a traditional lifestyle. He had run from it, sought adventure, and she knew it. Even before leaving for America, he had wanted her, but his restlessness had driven him away. No other woman would satisfy him, but he'd left anyway.

His thoughts returned to Boston—seeing her there. He hadn't been just angry, he had been enraged, but not because of her. *No*, he shook his head in self-disgust, *because of my own selfish needs. I left her behind.*

He knew what he wanted now. He wanted for her to be his wife, more than he could express in words. She'd haunted his dreams—her soft brown eyes, her moist lips on his, the way she'd returned his kisses.

She'd always been too selfless for her own good. And now she was fighting to gain her own position and stabilize her life. He hadn't told her that he was willing to stay in England and give up his wandering ways to be with her. That must be it. He had to try again. Let her know that he was willing to stay in England.

He stared off at the horizon. The sun was a mere slice above the distant mountain. He watched it disappear and darkness descend. He thought of living without Alaina, and he knew beyond doubt that he needed to be with her and if it meant giving up his life in Virginia, he would do it.

He had to make her see that.

He turned Jupiter about and rode back to the stables. He must talk to her, tonight.

As he dismounted and led Jupiter to the groom to be rubbed down, York appeared.

"Well, there you are, brother. I've been worried about you. Marielle told me that you and Alaina had a bit of a rift. Surprising, since the two of you can't keep your eyes off each other."

"What?" Martin growled and walked out of the stables, not wanting to talk to York about Alaina. His brother followed.

"I'm not blind, Martin. I've known for some time of your attraction to Alaina and of hers to you—you admitted that you wanted to marry the girl. Your fists clenched so tightly around the chair arms when I told you that Alaina was here, I thought you might jump from your seat to go and find her. I admire your ability to stifle your passion."

"Have I been so obvious?"

"Both you and Alaina have shown remarkable restraint. I have no idea what you argued about, but I think it's time you admitted your feelings for one another and got on with it."

"I asked her again to marry me," Martin admitted. "She refused, again."

"Perhaps you're going at it in the wrong way."

Martin stopped in his tracks and glared at York. "I told her how much I wanted to marry her. For God's sake, if she said she wanted to stay in England, I'd sell the land in Virginia." He heaved a sigh. "I didn't tell her that. I think that was my mistake." He leaned against a gatepost, realizing that he'd barked at his brother unnecessarily, rather than accept his own responsibility for his blundered proposals.

"Did you tell her you love her?"

Martin's chin dropped at York's question.

"I'd give up everything for her."

"Did you tell her you loved her? Martin, women need to hear the words."

Martin wrapped his arm around the gatepost and slumped against it.

York brought a hand to his brother's shoulder. "Admitting to love and saying the *word* is difficult, especially for us. Our parents gave us unconditional love and we lost them both too young. The pain that comes with loss can consume the soul."

"What are you talking about? Why are you bringing up the past?" Martin asked in a clipped, irritated tone.

"Because I believe you have built armor around your heart to protect yourself from ever experiencing pain that can cut through it."

"And you think you know what's inside me?"

"Yes," York nodded, his voice taking on a faraway quality as he looked out at the distant hills. "Because I can relate to what I see in you." He turned back to his brother. "I refused to allow myself to become so vulnerable that another could know what was in my heart. Better to remain detached, even cynical when it came to matters of the heart."

Martin's eyes fixed on his brother, who he'd always seen as strong and methodical, a man of action, without sentimentality or buttery words. Yet today when he watched him with his wife and his child, he'd seen a different side of him.

"It's Marielle then, she has softened your heart?"

York smiled. "Marielle met me at my worst. She managed to break through my defenses and I am eternally grateful. For you, it might be even more difficult to shed your armor. While Father spent his time grooming me for an earldom when I was barely old enough to sit upright on a pony, you were left at our mother's side. She adored you. When she died, you were barely ten years old. Do you remember how you cried in my arms?"

Martin looked away, feeling a twinge of awkwardness at the memory.

"I never saw you cry again. After what you must have perceived as weakness at her death you hardened, shielding your emotions. Loving and losing scars the soul. Allowing love in makes us vulnerable to the possibility of having to face that pain all over again. If something happened to Marielle, I don't know if I could go on. Yes, opening our hearts to love is a fearful thing but, brother," he paused until Martin's eyes met his, "loving is worth the risk. You need to share your true feelings with Alaina, as I have no doubt that you are very much in love with her."

Martin stared at York for a long time in disbelief. His brother, who had always seemed fearless to him, who had taught him how to overcome adversity, how to stay strong and to remain cool during the most harrowing situations, was advising him on love, even on how to woo a woman. He found himself grinning before reaching out and giving York a hard hug.

"Enough of that, brother," York said, cuffing Martin on the side of his head. "It's getting close to dinner and I'm hungry."

They walked back to the house together, pushing at each other, each obviously enjoying the camaraderie.

Martin realized that he'd been his own worst enemy. He loved Alaina with all his heart, yet he hadn't been able to speak the words or even admit them to himself. He'd convinced himself that he wanted to save her, protect her, bed her and desire her for the rest of his life.

A sudden thought caused him to choke up. What if he told her he loved her and she refused him again? Could he face the loss? He looked toward his brother and considered his words as they climbed the steps to the house.

Loving is worth the risk.

York left him in the foyer and went up to change for dinner. Martin started up the stairs but stopped. He'd waited long enough. He turned around and strode through the house, searching for Alaina. He found servants scurrying about and preparing the dinner table. He walked toward the larger drawing room and found it empty. He strode to the library and found a maid dusting a bookshelf. Swearing to himself, he checked the parlor where he thought he might find the ladies with their needlework.

Damn, he muttered. He walked backed toward the staircase. *Everyone must be dressing for dinner.* He marched up the stairs and stood at the top, wondering which bedchamber belonged to Alaina. He headed in the direction of the guest bedrooms most often prepared for guests.

He passed by two bedrooms with open doors. He could see that they were empty. He came to a closed door, nearly knocked, but looked farther down the hall to another closed door and decided that this one was most likely Cornelia's. She would be none too happy if she found him searching for Alaina in her bedchamber. Not that he really cared for appearances at the moment.

He walked to the end of the hall, recalling that it was the largest bedroom with a dramatic view of the gardens and the lake in the distance. He felt certain that his sister-in-law would have settled her in that room for her lengthy stay.

He rapped on the door.

"Yes?"

He gave a sigh of relief. It was Alaina's voice.

She opened the door slightly, her mouth dropping open at the sight of him. He pushed at the door, opening it farther and causing Alaina to step back. He walked into her bedchamber.

"Martin, this is inappropriate. Is something wrong?"

He could see she hadn't finished dressing. She clutched at the top of her gown, which had most likely not been secured in the back and gave him an inviting look at the swell of her breasts.

He remained still, staring at her, marveling to himself how beautiful she was and how much he loved this strong, courageous woman who had suffered much and refused to allow her hardships to keep her from going forward.

"Martin! You must leave!"

Her strong tone caused him to stop gawking and keep his mind on his mission.

"Alaina, much has been left unsaid between us."

"And you want to discuss it here, in my bedchamber. Please, allow me to finish dressing. I'll see you downstairs."

"No."

Alaina glared at him, appearing speechless. She reached for a shawl that hung over a chair and wrapped it around her.

He hadn't meant to scare her.

"What else needs to be said?" Alaina finally asked, after taking a few steps back and tying the shawl securely about her. "We are both moving on with our lives. I'll be leaving in a couple of days and you will be off to America. I truly wish you well, Martin."

He stepped closer to her. "My sweet Alaina," he whispered hoarsely.

She stepped back.

He drew closer.

She broke the silence. "You say we must talk and yet you stand there saying nothing. Perhaps I need to clear the air between us once and for all. Our personal relationship has been little more than a few stolen kisses. You have offered friendship and displayed unforgettable courage and sacrifice. Do not doubt that I am immensely grateful to you."

Martin opened his mouth to speak, but she raised a halting hand.

"Please, let me finish. I have a better sense of who I am, what I want, and what I need. Your willingness to marry me was honorable and as I've already said, unnecessary, though I deeply appreciate your desire to protect me. When you speak, I hear your love of the new world and I see it in your eyes. You have found a new homeland. I desire with all my heart for you to find happiness there."

"Alaina."

"I am not finished. Perhaps there *is* nothing more to be said. I understand now how important it is to believe in a dream and you should settle for nothing less. Before you left for America, I admit that in my foolishness, I saw the kiss we shared as a kiss of promise. I imagined that we might have a future together, but you needed to leave and follow your dream. We have both grown through our hardships and that is good, even if it means that we have grown apart."

"Alaina, *stop*." Martin forked his fingers through his hair and let out a harsh breath. "When I left England, I thought it was the best for both of us. I used the excuse that you needed time to grieve. You had gone through so much. I couldn't admit to myself that I was afraid, afraid of commitment, of what you stirred within me when I was near you. Better to escape."

"Afraid?" Her brows arched. "Martin Blackstone, afraid? Fear should have crumpled your spirit in the conditions you and your brother were forced to live in. Yet you demonstrated daring and bravery."

Martin grinned at the compliment. He reached over to her, lifted her hand to his lips and kissed her palm. "I learned not to allow fear of outside forces to cripple me." He swung an arm out toward one of the large windows. "I was more afraid of what was inside of me."

Alaina did not pull away from his touch, but allowed him to hold her hand, giving him the courage he needed to continue.

"Can you understand? I wanted you more than you could imagine, even before I left for the new world. But I knew you needed security and I couldn't offer that, at least not then. I felt out of control in your presence, Alaina. I didn't know how to cope with the kind of feelings you stirred within me. They scared me. I understood lust, but with you I felt more. I saw my family torn apart, the love my parents shared destroyed." He stopped, his eyes blurred. He rubbed them before staring up at the ceiling.

"And it was my father who had caused it all," Alaina said, lips trembling.

"You suffered from his tyranny as well. Both York and I knew that. My running off to America had to do with my own issues. The thought of committing my life to another brought up the fear that I would lose what I had found." He paused, looked into her eyes and rubbed a finger gently against the softness of her cheek. "I learned how to get out of dangerous situations, situations that were confining in any way. I ran from uncomfortable feelings and from you."

Alaina looked stunned at his admission. He

paused, knowing he had caught her by surprise. He opened his mouth to say more, but she raised her hand to stop him.

"In Boston, I saw your disgust of what I had done," she said finally, lowering her eyes. "I didn't know if you could possibly understand why I acted as I did, why I was willing to cast aside my reputation, my virtue."

"Alaina." Martin grasped her shoulders and urged her to look at him. "I never felt disgust toward you. I was in awe that you would sacrifice yourself to save your brother's reputation, even his life. I wanted to say more to you then, but I was so angry that you'd placed yourself in such danger. I was angry at myself. While I was off to find myself in America, a scoundrel was able to use your vulnerability against you to do his bidding. I left you unprotected. I shall never forgive myself."

"It wasn't your place to protect me, Martin. You owed me nothing."

"But you are wrong. My cowardice allowed a stranger to compromise you." He paused. "To take away your innocence." Martin stopped, he could see he upset her. "Alaina, why are you looking away, are you all right?" He turned her face toward his and could see the tears running down her cheek.

"Please don't cry. I am doing it again, hurting you."

"No, Martin. I misunderstood. When I felt your anger toward me, I was so humiliated, ashamed."

"My beautiful Alaina." He took her face in both his hands. "Forgive me if I caused you to feel such pain. I thought of you every day I was in America and every night. I couldn't escape my feelings for you. I planned to return to you before I knew of what you'd done. If you would find it unbearable to come to America with me, I understand. After all, it would be a hard life and asking that of you is selfish. You deserve a life of gentility. I'll sell the land in Virginia. It was probably just a foolish dream anyway. I'll stay in England, if you'll consent to be my wife."

Martin rubbed a tear away that rolled down her cheek. "What are you thinking? Forgive my clumsiness. My words aren't meant to make you cry."

Alaina lifted her eyes to his. "I want you to know that Harrington did not want to take a chance that I would refuse to carry through with the charade or present a respectable public image as his fiancée. He never tried to take advantage of me in that way and though the chaperones he provided were *unusual*, we were seldom alone together."

Martin raised a brow. He had jumped to conclusions, assumed that Harrington had taken her virtue. Despite his embarrassment, he couldn't help feeling relieved.

"Regardless, it wouldn't change my feelings, you know." He wrapped his arms around her and looked into her eyes. "Alaina, I love you."

She pulled back and stared at him, her lips trembling. "You love me? Oh, Martin, how I have waited for you to say those words." She reached a hand up to touch his face. "I have loved you for so long."

Martin's lips spread into wide grin. "And will you marry me, my love?"

Her face glowed as she returned his smile and spoke the word he'd prayed she'd say.

"Yes."

Martin saw a world of love in her eyes and heard it in her simple utterance. Before another word could escape her lips, he picked her up, twirled her around and let out a howl.

"Martin! Everyone will come running," Alaina gasped, her voice choked with laughter.

"We will marry, have dozens of children."

"Dozens? Is your plantation in Virginia to be so large?"

Martin brought her to a stop, his eyes delving into hers. "You'll live in America? Are you certain?"

Alaina nodded. "Wherever you are, my love, I will be."

Epilogue

"KATHERINE WILL be almost two years old before we see you again, Alaina. I don't know how I shall stand it," Marielle exclaimed with a sigh.

Holding back tears, Alaina tried to respond but the words caught in her throat. The past few months had been a heaven of special moments beyond her wildest dreams. Now, as she and Martin stood on the Liverpool dock preparing to board a ship to America, she felt a mixture of sadness and exhilaration.

Everyone she loved most in the world had come to see them off. Even little Katherine was included. The child stretched her pudgy arms out to her as York, her new brother-in-law, attempted to hold his daughter snugly in his arms. When Alaina drew near she showered her with wet kisses.

Richard gave her a big hug and promised to come and visit in a few months time. Aunt Cornelia stood off to the side, dabbing her eyes.

Martin, seeing Alaina's tears, came immediately to her side. "You can change your mind right now," he whispered. "I could not ask for more happiness than what we've shared together since our marriage. We'll stay in England. You only have to say the word."

"And cause you to be a proper English gentleman? Heavens, no." Seeing her husband's excitement each time he talked about his dreams was happiness enough. They had talked for hours since their marriage about the land he'd purchased. She doubted that he'd left out even the smallest detail. He told her of the orange and violet sunsets, the mountains that seemed to embrace the land that was now his. He described the house they would live in that would be nearly completed when they arrived.

He wanted her to choose the colors, arrange the furniture, some of which they'd already purchased in London and was being shipped. Even York and Marielle added their suggestions during their many discussions. She thought of the letters sent back and forth between him and his overseer that contained news of progress being made, down to the acquisitions of livestock and even flowers and fruit trees to adorn the gardens.

She couldn't help being as excited as Martin to set sail and arrive at their new home in Virginia. He'd thought she would prefer to stay in England but she'd reminded him that her life in her homeland had not always been a happy one. Yes, she would miss her brother and her dear friends, and it was true that her time in Boston could not be completely erased from her memory, but a more hope-filled future was before her. She recalled the excitement she'd witnessed of travelers ready to begin a new life in America. She remembered how their dreams of a new future appeared to overshadow their fears. She was more than ready. She understood there would be some hardships but she was with the man she loved and who loved her in return. She could ask for no more.

As they prepared to board, she reached out to Marielle and Aunt Cornelia and hugged them once more, each of them wiping away tears.

"Martin, I don't know how long our wives will be able to stay apart," York said as Katharine squirmed in his arms, letting him know that she, too, wanted to join the ladies.

"We shall be back for a visit, maybe in a year, that is, if Alaina is up to a long voyage."

York gave his brother a questioning glance.

Martin grinned. "I don't plan on waiting too long before this little one has a new baby cousin." Martin gently pinched Katherine's button nose before reaching into the women's cluster and tugging Alaina away.

"Darling, it's time to board. Are you ready for our new adventure?"

Alaina nodded and smiled. *Our new adventure.* She loved the sound of it, loved that they would share this one together.

Yes, she was ready.

Thank you for reading *A Kiss of Promise*! If you enjoyed it, please help others find it by writing an Amazon review. I can't begin to tell you how important reviews are to authors and how appreciated. I hope you will also sign up for my newsletter to hear about new releases, win free books, and more, on my website www.elaineviolette.com.

Here's a sneak peak at my newest historical, The Diary of Narcissa Dunn.

The Diary of Narcissa Dunn
Elaine Violette

Chapter One

Spring 1826

Hmmm hmm hmmm hmm

A smile played on Olivia's lips but faded as her eyelids fluttered and she became fully awake. Startled, she lifted her head and glanced around her bedroom. "A dream, only a dream," she mumbled, sinking back into her pillow. She closed her eyes, hoping to recapture a vision of the mysterious woman humming a tune as sweet as a lullaby, but the memory flickered and disappeared into the world of dreams.

Tossing back her covers, she sat up, disturbing her cat who had been taking a long stretch at the foot of the bed. "It appears we've slept too long this morning, Speckles." With a yawn, Olivia smoothed a hand over the cat's gray and white spotted coat until a rapping on her door caused Speckles to jump from the bed and scoot under it.

"Livie, you best get your bottom out of bed before your father gets back from the barn. He been gone over an hour. You know it take him half the time it takes you to get ready for church."

Being Sunday, Olivia wasn't surprised at the intrusion or the maid's scolding words clearly heard through the closed door. "I'm awake, Lovena. Be down shortly."

"You need to get some food in you before sittin' through one more of your daddy's long sermons. Get a move on."

"I'll be dressed and ready." Olivia called out with a yawn as she swept her thick, nearly black curls from her face and touched her feet to the cold wood floor. As she made up her bed and fluffed her pillow, she heard the customary sound of the housemaid's heavy shoes clomping down the stairs.

A spark of recollection from the strange dream returned as she poured water from her pitcher into a small basin. She'd sensed a deep sadness in the woman. *Maybe there's someone in our church who needs prayers*. She tried to recall the woman's features but she'd remained in shadows just as in previous dreams.

"Who is she?" Olivia wondered aloud as she immersed her hands into the cold water. Splashing her face helped her snap out of the remnants of a poor night's sleep and the lingering dream.

When she finished washing, she dressed quickly. The sun's reflection on her mirror as she brushed through her hair reminded her of her lateness. She tied the thick unruly curls back with a ribbon. After taking one last look in the mirror, she stepped into her shoes, laced them quickly and hurried downstairs.

Her father, the town's Congregational minister, refused to listen to any excuse for being late for church. He liked to greet his congregation as they walked through the meetinghouse doors. Olivia never minded the hours spent at church. Her father's sermons were always well prepared and even though his messages were ones she'd listened to at the dinner table many times, she didn't mind hearing them again. He still had a great booming voice, though he'd grown grayer and paunchier in the last few years.

When she entered the small breakfast room, her father was dressed in his Sunday suit with his worn Bible beside him. He lifted his eyes to his daughter, his expression sending a disapproving message at her late arrival. Lovena gave her a knowing glance as she set down a basket of warm biscuits to add to the thick slices of country bacon and scrambled eggs she'd already served.

"I won't be able to fit into my trousers, Lovena, if you keep serving these hearty meals. You make enough for ten," Reverend Fuller said as he reached for a biscuit.

"Who knows who gonna stop in any time mornin' or night? Young Mr. Tapley don't seem to think he needs an invite anymore," Lovena said, shaking her scarf-wrapped head that concealed her gray nappy hair.

"William has become part of the family over the past few months. I am impressed with him," he countered. "He takes his studies seriously and seeks my guidance, though I doubt I'm the reason for his frequent visits." Raising a brow, he smiled at Olivia who sat opposite him.

Olivia took a large bite of a buttered biscuit hoping to avoid another discussion of William's merits. Her father was especially pleased William not only came from a well-respected family in town but he'd be ordained in a couple of months. Since her father planned to retire soon, he appeared to have his eyes on William as his successor to the pulpit.

"He is an honorable young man, Olivia, and he'll make a decent living as a minister." He paused to take a sip of tea. "I believe he'll ask me for your hand soon."

Olivia could no longer ignore her father's piercing gaze over the lip of his cup. Marriage was far from her mind. Only a year and a few months had passed since her mother's death. "I look forward to spending more time with you before I think of marriage."

"I appreciate the sentiment but you're of an age to consider your future. William's twenty-five. He wants to be settled down before taking on the responsibilities of a congregation. You could hardly do better than with a man of the cloth." Winking at his daughter, he lifted his Bible and held it to his chest as he so often did when he was preaching.

Olivia pursed her lips rather than be drawn into his attempt at humor. She might agree if she fell in love with someone as Godly as her father. She knew William was much admired by other girls in town, but she felt no passion in his presence. True, nineteen was a marriageable age but she wasn't ready for such a commitment. Apart from her church duties, she looked forward to helping out at the local school in the fall. Picking up a bacon slice, she bit into it, hoping her father would resume his own breakfast.

"Lovena, will you be going over to Reverend Baylor's house later?" the minister asked, rising from his chair and pushing it into place.

"Not `till noon today."

"I understand his parlor may be getting too small for your church meetings."

"We sure is cozy in there. Reverend Baylor's been talkin' about startin' a fund to build a Baptist church but, Lordy, I be dead before that come about."

"No need to think so dismally. The Lord provides. Olivia, you'll need your cloak today," he said, addressing her without turning around. "There's a chill in the air. I'll be waiting on the porch. Don't dally."

Olivia stared at her father's back as he walked out the kitchen door that led onto the side porch. Standing now, she accepted the cloak and bonnet Lovena held out to her. She didn't miss the sympathetic look on the maid's round face.

BENJAMIN STOOD looking up at the Fuller's old barn

and its adjacent structure. His instructions were to tear down the section that once housed servants and farmhands and use the wood not yet rotted to repair the barn. Uncle Sylvester bartered Ben's labor to the church during the slow months in return for wood, nails, and other commodities needed to run his shop. Since the weather improved daily, it wasn't a bad part time job though he much preferred working in his uncle's carpentry shop.

His uncle wanted him to take over the business someday and had put a hammer in Ben's hand as soon as he was old enough to hold one. Now as his apprentice, Ben was learning every aspect of the carpentry trade. Uncle Sylvester, or Uncle Syl as he called him, taught him about the different types of wood and how to carve and smooth each piece to perfection. It was as if the wood axed from tree trunks came alive again under his uncle's master hand. He wanted to do the same. Being covered with splinters and sawdust in the morning and cleaning up for an afternoon of polishing wood to a satin finish was a great day's work but in late winter and early spring, business was slow. Except for staining a piece of furniture or making a coffin when needed, new jobs had been sparse.

Walking through the open barn doors, Ben gazed around the enclosed area one last time before preparing to leave for the day. The smooth hand hewn timbers and post and beam structure of the barn impressed him. It had been built well to withstand New England winters. Removing some old boards and patching up the roof would keep it sturdy for a few more years.

The barn was no longer used to house cattle or large farming equipment but areas needed cleaning up and re-structuring to meet Reverend Fuller's expectations. The minister wanted the barn renovated as a carriage house, keeping a couple of stalls for the horses and bartering off unneeded farm tools and machinery. Tools for planting and harvesting, horse and carriage needs, as well as bins to feed the horses and chickens would be cleaned up and refurbished.

The minister was a fair man, though he wasn't too pleased Ben had chosen to evaluate the job this morning rather than attend the long hours in church. He at least understood Ben's hours might not be regular, especially if one of his uncle's jobs needed his immediate attention. Simply overseeing his week's accomplishments and not carrying out heavy work on the Lord's Day seemed to appease Reverend Fuller. Ben much preferred walking the fields on a Sunday morning or riding his horse to Snipsic Lake, the "Snip", as most called it. He liked to toss in a line and talk to God on his own terms.

Watching Olivia Fuller leave for church this morning with her father was the highlight of Ben's morning. She had striking beauty and a willowy figure to match. Today she was wrapped in a deep purple cape and wore an ivory-colored bonnet, her thick curls spilling down her back. She looked beautiful. Would he have an opportunity to talk to her one of these days? Even a simple 'good morning' would do. He might recognize a disagreeable manner that would cause him to release her from his thoughts. He hoped so since now that her father hired him, he needed to keep his mind on his work and not on the minister's daughter.

How many years had he admired her from a distance? He doubted she ever noticed him though they were in the same school room for a time. He'd been a scrawny kid wearing trousers with holes worn into the knees and attended school only when he wasn't needed for farm work. Olivia, on the other hand, was always well dressed and perfectly groomed. Fortunately, Ben's uncle was his best teacher and what he didn't learn in class, Uncle Syl made sure he learned at home.

Why was he wasting his time thinking about Miss Fuller? The news circulating around town rumored she was practically engaged to Will Tapley who wasn't one of Ben's favorite people.

He walked outside and decided to do a last check of the small adjoining rooms. From what he'd observed from the inner barn wall, the attached section appeared to be barely tacked on with few crudely tapered iron nails and was most likely built quickly out of necessity rather than from careful planning.

A door to the right of the larger barn doors led into a dank, narrow hall that ran the length of the side of the barn. As he walked down the hallway, he took a quick glance into each of the three small rooms. It was obvious the old living quarters hadn't been occupied for years and no one took the time to clean them out from their previous tenants.

Entering the last room, he looked about,

grimacing. Two sets of bunks with moldy mattresses stained with dirt and rodent feces were left to decay. What appeared to be rags or old blankets were heaped in a corner. The middle room was smaller and in similar condition, except it held one cot with a shredded mattress hanging half off the bed. The mattress' filthy stuffing was pulled out and strewn about the floor. A couple of empty drawers were heaped on top of each other without a chest to contain them. As in the other room, long, crudely made nails were hammered into a wall and must have served as a place to hang work clothes or coats. Both of the rooms had a small side window with cracked panes covered in cobwebs and dead insects.

When he walked into the front room, he noted the larger window that looked out at the main house a few hundred feet away. A moldy candle, its holder caked with dead spiders, sat on the window sill. Pressed against the front wall was a small cot with rusted springs and a filthy mattress in the same rotting condition as the others. A broken drawer lay on the floor. In a corner, an old wooden rocker sat with cobwebs snarled about its vertical rungs. Crumpled on its seat, lay a moth-eaten wool blanket. As he looked up and studied the support beams above, a creaking noise caused him to shoot a glance toward the rocking chair. It moved slightly, then stilled. Had a mouse skittered by?

Enough for today, he decided.

He wasn't looking forward to working through the cobwebs and filth before tearing this whole section down, but it had to be done. Once it was razed, he'd set aside salvageable boards and use them to repair the barn, a more constructive job that would give him some sense of accomplishment.

Relieved to be back outside, he breathed in the fresh spring air and brushed off cobwebs clinging to his sleeves and pants. Tomorrow he'd start shoveling out the side rooms. Taking a last look around, he returned to the barn, pushed the large doors closed and bolted them.

"You keep walkin' 'round the barn, Benjamin, like you been doin' and you gonna get dizzy."

Ben turned to see Lovena, the Fullers' housemaid, smiling at him, her arms crossed under her full aproned bosom. He tipped his worn cap and returned the smile.

"The Reverend Fuller and his daughter are off to church. They left behind a table full of food I ain't about to waste. Come in for some nice warm biscuits and my strawberry preserves before you figure out what you gonna do with that ramshackle barn."

"I'm obliged ma'am. I've heard you're one of the best cooks in town. I'm not about to say no."

"Well, come on now."

Ben walked with her toward the farmhouse.

"I been telling the reverend those horses are gonna have the roof fallin' in on them if he don't get the old barn fixed. With the wind and rain goin' through there in the coldest months, it ain't fit for an old raccoon to live in, never mind those two fine horses he got in there."

"No doubt he heard you. He hired me to whip it back into shape though I can't promise much. I'll close up the holes as best I can."

"He says you gonna rip out those old rooms."

'Those are my instructions, ma'am."

"You call me Lovena, like everybody else."

When they reached the house, he followed her up the side porch steps and into the kitchen. Once inside, she signaled him to take a seat in the breakfast room.

"I'll be right back with some tea. You help yourself."

Ben took a biscuit from a basket on the table and scooped jam on it as he looked around the small area sectioned off from the larger kitchen and painted a warm beige. Except for a side board, the room held just the wood table and four chairs. An open doorway led to a larger dining room. From his vantage point, it appeared more elegant, with beige and dark blue striped wallpaper. An ornate gold mirror on the wall reflected a dark wood dining table beyond it with a vase of spring flowers set in the center. His observations were interrupted when Lovena walked in carrying a tray with a teapot and cups.

"Before the missus had me move in the back room here, I lived in those drafty rooms you be tearing down," she said, setting the tray down on the table. "Mrs. Fuller wanted me nearer to the kitchen so I didn't waste no time gettin' busy. She was one bossy lady, always..." She stopped, slapping a hand to her cheek. "Listen to me goin' on. Good Lord, I shouldn't be talkin' against the dead. Anyways, I think those rooms are haunted. You be careful. Those damp walls have frightenin' stories to tell. I don't go near 'em, no way, no more." Lovena rubbed goose bumps appearing on her heavy brown arms. "No way, I say. You be careful."

As Lovena poured his tea, Ben raised a brow at her superstition. The house had been built by Reverend Fuller's father in the early 1700's, he'd been told. Ben guessed the barn and adjoining quarters were slightly newer but not by much. He enjoyed learning about the history of the older homes and their designs. More were being built in town in the Georgian style with Federal and Greek revival features. His uncle enjoyed teaching him the specific characteristics of each house along the main road. Ben hoped to build his own one day so he carefully noted the features that interested him most.

Though the town was mostly farm land, some of the older homes had interesting histories. Despite slavery being outlawed in the late 1700s in Connecticut, a few landowners still enslaved domestics and towns kept a blind eye. This house had stayed in the family and being a religious one, he wasn't about to believe some disgruntled spirit, slave or free, chose those rundown rooms to haunt.

Lovena looked the young man over as he reached for another biscuit. He was tall, slim, and broad shouldered with a light complexion, reddened by the sun and a sprinkle of freckles across the bridge of his nose. Muscled arms caused the material on his faded flannel sleeves to pull taut when he creased his elbows. She guessed he was in his early twenties.

Good lookin' boy and polite, she thought, returning to the kitchen to finish cleaning up from breakfast, *not like that uppity, pasty-faced Will Tapley who don't give a nod or a thank you though he shows up for dinner more times than I can count. He ain't the one for my Olivia. Not with those thin lips and bushy eyebrows. They meet like squirrels' tails touchin' when he's listenin' to the reverend talk religion.*

Not that her opinion mattered, though she'd been with the family for close to thirty years. She figured she'd gone past fifty some time ago but she had no birth certificate to prove it. Her bones told her she was old. What did matter was being here. She'd been with Olivia since she was born and the girl needed her, especially with Mrs. Fuller gone.

The minister's time was taken up by church business and Olivia was expected to serve the church just as her mother had done, taking part in Bible studies, working with the choir and playing the organ, not to mention her home chores. Olivia could only do so much and the minister could ill afford to hire another maid.

My sweet Livie, she thought, remembering the day the child had come running into the kitchen and saw Lovena leaning over a pail of water with blood dripping from a cut finger.

Lovena, you're bleeding!

No harm done chile. I just got sloppy slicin' up peppers.

Your blood…it's the same color as mine when I fell on the stones outside.

We is all the same on the inside, honey. Our hearts the same too. Don't you forget chile, we is all the same in God's eyes.

She hid a grin with her palm as she recalled how little Livie's eyes widened and the child reached up and gave Lovena the biggest hug a little girl could give. She was the one who gave the child hugs. Her mother was stern and tended toward coldness with strict expectations for her daughter. She loved the child, the maid knew, but she was hard on her, always expecting her to behave perfectly, especially in front of others. Her father had bowed to his wife's wishes concerning the child. Only Lovena would allow her to play like a little one should when the reverend and his missus weren't about.

"Thank you, ma'am, for your hospitality."

Lovena pulled herself from her daydreaming, realizing she'd gone off into the past and forgot about the young man who now stood by the back door cap in hand.

"My name's Lovena, Benjamin, and you remember what I said about those rooms."

"I'll keep it in mind and if I run into any spirits, I'll be sure to send them packing."

"Go on, now." She shooed him off with the striped dish towel she held in her hand.

Grinning, Ben tipped his cap and left.

Such a nice young man. Been well brought up by his uncle. As he disappeared down the side porch steps, Lovena's expression grew grim. She peered through the window at the old red barn with its quartered-off spaces built to house the help. She thought of the heartbreak that once lived in those drafty rooms and a shiver coursed through her.

WHEN BEN arrived the next afternoon, this time with his horse hitched to a wagon, he was surprised to see Olivia sitting in front of an easel on the back lawn. He brought the wagon to a halt in front of the barn. Jumping down, he stood wavering between walking over to introduce himself or getting to work and avoiding her.

He didn't have to think for long. She caught his eye and waved.

"It's now or never," he muttered, pushing his hands into his trouser pockets. He strode over and removed his hat. "Good day, Miss Fuller. My name's Benjamin Pratt. Folks call me Ben."

Olivia chuckled. "I know who you are, though it's true we have never been properly introduced. Father told me you would be working here."

Ben was surprised she'd noticed his presence at all. "I'll be here most afternoons for a while. I work with my uncle mornings."

"Carpentry, I understand." She looked up at him with an arm across her forehead to block the sun's glare.

He nodded. So she knew more about him than he'd expected.

"Do you design and carve furniture or just build it?"

Ben laughed.

"Is my question amusing? Perhaps I offended. I see carpentry as an admirable trade."

"No offense taken. I build furniture and I

suppose I have a knack for wood carving." He shrugged his shoulders and gave her a teasing grin. "My uncle is gifted in creating traditional European designs. He enjoys passing on his knowledge. Most customers seem to prefer a plainer style and it's less expensive."

Olivia smiled at him. She looked too pretty. The cotton ruffle of her bonnet framed her face and emphasized her dark brown eyes. Her voice was as pleasant as her expression. His admiration nearly caused him to take in the sound without absorbing her words.

"Fine carpentry is certainly an art and much admired when furniture is well made. My mother took great pride in pieces brought from England by my grandparents."

He nodded, pleased she appreciated the trade. "They are lasting legacies of fine craftsmen from past eras. I have no desire to do anything else." He drew his eyes to her painting. "You're talented. The flowers look alive as if I could touch them; even feel the softness of those petals."

"Thank you." For a moment she held his gaze.

"Well, I'd better get busy or your father may complain to my uncle that I am loafing on the job."

"It's nice to meet you."

"Enjoy the sunshine, Miss Fuller."

"Olivia."

He nodded, hoping he didn't appear like a sick-in-love school boy. He walked toward the barn, pulling his cap back on. *Olivia*, he thought. *She's not simply beautiful. She's intelligent and observant and her voice...* He pulled at the latch on

the barn door, walked in and forked his hand
through his hair. He blew out a breath to temper
his body's heated reaction to a simple conversation.
"The rooms, focus on those gloomy rooms."

Author's Note

I appreciate hearing from my readers on Facebook. If you'd like news of upcoming books, please visit and sign up for my mailing list on my website at www.elaineviolette.com or message me on Facebook.com/Elaine.Violette.author.

Other Books by Elaine

Regal Reward   (Book One: Blackstone Brother's Rise and Fall)
A Convenient Pretense (a Regency Romance)
The Diary of Narcissa Dunn   (Book One of Redemption series)

Coming Soon:
Seeds of Hope (Book Two of Redemption Series)

.................................About Elaine Violette

Elaine is a Golden Heart Finalist (NJRW) and has received outstanding reviews for her historical romances. She is a veteran English teacher and holds a BS in English Education from the University of CT and an MS in Educational Leadership from Central CT State University. She presently teaches public speaking part time at a local community college. She is a member of Romance Writers of America and CT Romance Writers (CTRWA). She resides on the Connecticut shoreline with her golfing husband, Drew, and delights in being a wife, mother, and grandmother.